J
See   c 1

Seely, Debra

Grasslands

Grasslands

Grasslands

by
Debra Seely

Holiday House/*New York*

Acknowledgments

This book could never have been written without the stories from my great-grandfather, A.V. Fink, my great-grandmother, Rowena Fink, and my grandparents, George and Dorothy Fieser. Thanks also to my parents, Ken and Lois Short, for their stories and support.

Thank you to Richard Spilman, Margaret Dawe, Craig Miner, Diane Quantic, Sarah Daugherty, James Wilcox, and Betty Pesetsky for their guidance; to Clare Vanderpool and Joan Heck Spilman for their careful reading and their ideas; and to Essie Sappenfield, Bryan Dietrich, Jerome Stueart, Mary Saionz, Christine Jensen, John Jenkinson, Lise Goett, Melissa Stanton, Gordon Houser, Glenn Fisher, Julia Dagenais, Nathan Filbert, Rusty Smoker, Mary Goodwin, Aaron Leis, Mary Seitz, Jim Canning, David Cullen, and the Milton Center at Newman University.

For their suggestions and time, thanks to Cindy Cisneros-McGilvray, Kimi Matumura, Nathan Hittle, Garrick Enright, and the folks in Mrs. C-Mac's seventh-grade classes.

The Old Cowtown Museum in Wichita, the Sedgwick County Historical Museum, the Mennonite Heritage Museum, and the Kansas State Historical Society all provided information and examples that were helpful to this story.

Thank you to Sarah Bagby, Bruce Jacobs, and Watermark Books for their helpful encouragement and suggestions, and to Harold and Fran Fieser for their ranching and farming input.

To my agent, Jodie Rhodes, thanks for her enthusiasm and persistence. Many thanks to Regina Griffin and the editors at Holiday House.

Most importantly, thank you to Dave Seely for his love, help, and support, and thanks to Michael, Elise, and Matthew Seely for being there during this book's writing.

Library of Congress Cataloging-in-Publication Data
Seely, Debra.
Grasslands / Debra Seely.—1st ed.
p.   cm.
Summary: In the 1880s, thirteen-year-old Thomas moves west from the aristocratic Virginia home of his grandparents to a poor Kansas farm to live with a father he barely remembers and his new stepfamily.
ISBN 0-8234-1731-X (hardcover)
[1. Frontier and pioneer life—Kansas—Fiction.
2. Kansas—History—19th century—Fiction.   3. Stepfamilies—Fiction.
4. Moving, Household—Fiction.]   I. Title.

PZ7.S4518 Gr 2002
[Fic]—dc21   2002017144

In memory of
A. V. Fink

Chapter 1

The letter came to my grandparents' house while I was at school, in a fistfight.

At recess, while the girls took turns on the rope swing under the hickory, the boys played crack the whip. I was the whip. A boy I didn't cotton to, Roy Fitch, whined that I cracked sharp enough to pull his arm bone out of the socket. I said I wasn't breaking any rules, and he said, "When did your family ever worry about rules?"

"You watch your mouth, Fitch."

"You know your grandfather is a rich man's judge," he said, and I punched him in the nose. A crowd closed around us. "You motherless . . . ," he hollered, and swung at me.

He missed. I threw him into the dust and landed a good blow to his ear. I managed another to his chin before the teacher ran out and broke up the fight.

I was not a bully. To tell the truth, I felt sorry for the boy, even though I didn't like him, because my grandfather had ruled against his father and cost the man his life savings. But I was not one to dodge a fight. Believing as I did in the Code of the West, I had to defend this slur on my family, especially the mention of my mother. The gang in the schoolyard, all of them experts in matters of school warfare, agreed I won with no trouble.

I followed this code the more firmly because I didn't exactly understand it. If pressed, I would have said something about standing up for right, not shooting a man in the back, any of the phrases that came from the dime novels I sneaked into my room and read by candle late at night. The West was a thousand miles away, and although at thirteen I had definite notions about it, none of them came from my experience.

I had made one westward journey, as a baby in a covered wagon, with a storage crate for a cradle. I got packed back to Virginia before I could talk. Besides that, I had only cowboy and outlaw games in the blue-green woods, and, of course, the schoolyard.

* * *

After school, I swaggered up the dirt lane toward my grandparents' farm at the top of the hill, throwing shadow punches toward the meadow boxed in by trees, where my old pony grazed. I called to him, "Rustler's coming!" but he just raised his head, snorted, and went back to chewing grass.

So I went on, bowing to a buggy I grandly allowed to pass. Lines from *The Pilgrim's Progress*, which our class had that day finished studying, hummed in my head. *The Pilgrim's Progress* bored me. We'd had to memorize and recite parts of it, which bored me even more, but I'd liked one verse:

> *O let the pilgrims, let the pilgrims then*
> *Be vigilant, and quit themselves like men.*

Pilgrims were seekers, like the cowboys in my novels, vigilant, on the lookout for trouble. And I liked the idea of being able to "quit" myself like a man, particularly in a fistfight.

The dogwoods bloomed, and the air was sweet with their scent. I jumped the porch steps, feeling good, and burst into the hallway.

But when I saw my grandparents standing together in the parlor, I tried to cover the blood on my shirt with my vest, because, Code of the West or not, I would get punished for fighting.

My grandfather held a sheet of paper. He stopped talking to my grandmother and frowned at me.

"What happened to your shirt?" Grandfather asked. He already knew the answer, so I didn't bother to lie. I dropped my books on the bench by the door and joined them in the parlor, running my fingers along the glass-fronted bookcase beside the fireplace. My grandfather's law books sat behind the glass, dark-colored and somber.

"I had to," I said. "A boy called you a rich man's judge." I could have fibbed about the cause of the fight, but I wanted Grandfather to know what people said about him.

"A gentleman doesn't settle his differences with his fists. When will you learn that?"

I bowed my head and waited for the rest of the usual lecture, but it didn't come. Instead, Grandfather shifted the paper from one hand to the other and cleared his throat. I raised my eyes, watched his face, his set lips, looking for clues.

At last he spoke. "Thomas, what do you remember of your father?"

I didn't remember my father. My father never wrote to me or to my sister. We would get post-cards at Christmas, brightly colored drawings of cowboys on horses, or of charging buffalo, and on the other side, only my father's signature. When I thought of my father, I thought of these postcards. He lived on a farm in Kansas, and I imagined he was like the men in the pictures. When I was little, five or six, I had drawn my own pictures of cow-boys and buffalo and sent them to my father, but I hadn't done that for a long time, because he never wrote back and the pictures started to seem a childish thing to do.

I had one memory, a half-remembered shadow that might have been a dream, only I knew it wasn't. Someone long ago was holding my hand, pointing to my grandparents' house and saying, "That was your mama's house." I was dressed in clothes that scratched, and I had been on a train, but I couldn't put a face with the voice. It might have been my father. I liked to think it was.

"I just remember the postcards at Christmas," I told my grandfather.

With his white hair and creased face, my grandfather always looked grave. Only his eyes could give him away, and they were somber now. My stomach clutched. Had something happened to my father?

"Come into the dining room," Grandfather said. "This letter has some news."

Grandmother brought me a slice of the cherry pie that her colored cook, Helen, had made that day. We sat at the oak table. Grandfather cleared his throat.

"Did he die?" I asked quickly, before Grandfather could begin to speak.

"No, he's alive. And well." Grandfather frowned, and I could tell he was forming the words in his head. If my father wasn't dead, I couldn't imagine what else could be so important. "You were born here in Virginia, Thomas. I want you to remember that your roots are here," Grandfather said finally. "Your family went out to Kansas only because your papa couldn't make a go of anything around here after the war." He cleared his throat again. "But I don't know as he's prospered in Kansas after all these years. I still don't know what your mother saw in him." Grandmother shook her head, to warn Grandfather not to talk against my father in front of me.

"At any rate, he brought you and your sister back here to be with your own people, after your mother died. We all thought it was for the best, to give you a sense of your own place and traditions, rather than let you grow up wild in that place, with no mother to teach you."

Grow up wild. That phrase went right through me, causing a wonderful shiver. What kind of boy would I have been had I stayed out there, with my father? I was burning to know what was in that letter.

"Thomas, it seems your father has married again."

This was not the news I wanted. I jabbed my fork into a fat cherry, watched it burst. "Why? When?"

"The thing is, son, he married her a year ago. She's a widow, and, ah, there are three children—"

"They live there, with him?" I heard my voice get shrill. "He waited a whole year to tell us?"

"It seems he waited until now to let us know because he wanted to be able to offer this other piece of news. It's not exactly news, more of an invitation."

My heart began to beat hard. "What kind of invitation?"

"For you and your sister." Grandfather's eyes searched my face. "He wants you to come live with them in Kansas."

The room was still. Larks sang in the birch tree outside the window. "Have you told Becky?"

"I wrote to her at the academy," Grandmother said. Becky attended Silverthorn Academy for Young Women, ten miles from my grandparents' farm outside of Youngstown. I was supposed to go to the nearby Wright Academy in the fall.

"Becky has only a year left," Grandfather said. "She won't want to interrupt her studies. I haven't heard of any private academies out West." He rubbed his jaw. "Your grandmother and I are not in favor of disrupting your education, either, Thomas. College would be out of the question if you don't go to the academy."

"I want to go west," I said flatly, not looking at my grandparents. I studied my pie, pushed a cherry back and forth across the roses on the china plate.

Grandmother and Grandfather glanced at each other again. "Well, we don't have to decide right away," Grandmother said.

I left the table. At the entrance to the parlor, I stopped. Inside, beside the horsehair settee, was a round cherry table with daguerreotypes on top. Somber-faced people stared at me from silver frames. I reached for the picture of my mother and father. It had been taken shortly after they married, several years before they left for Kansas. They stood together, unsmiling. My mother had light hair pulled into two smooth braids knotted in the back in a big bun. Her eyes were light too, large and kind-looking. She wore a white blouse with a high collar and an opal brooch at the neck. Becky kept that brooch upstairs in her jewelry box.

I usually studied only my mother's face, going over every soft, familiar line. My father's face was more complicated. The hair was dark, like mine, and the eyes shadowed, making their expression hard to read. High cheekbones, like mine, cast shadows on the face as well. A stiff, high collar without any kind of tie clutched at his throat, and a dark suit coat covered his chest. He had a full, dark mustache above his upper lip that gave him, I decided now, an air of daring. My father looked like the kind of man who would not be stuck inside reading *The Pilgrim's Progress* while dogwoods were blooming.

I picked up my books and jumped the stairs three at a time. What if I never had to worry about scratching the mahogany banister again? Never had to worry about knocking over a vase or breaking my grandmother's china?

In my room, instead of studying, I stretched out on my bed and stared up at the ceiling. I tried to recall something more about my father. But there was nothing besides the dim memory of the voice saying, "That was your mama's house." I tried to decide if the voice had been kind or stern, the hand that had held mine rough or soft, but it was no use.

I rose and sat down at the pine desk Grandfather had made for me. In the single drawer he had put a false bottom. I took paper and pen out of the drawer and removed the panel. Ten thin, paper-bound volumes lay beneath. The drawings on the covers showed cowboys on horseback, trains belching black smoke, Indians with bows poised to shoot. Grandfather didn't approve of these novels, so I had to hide them, but the Western men in them, Buffalo Bill Cody and Dick Deadeye, had real adventures, shooting wild animals, fighting desperate enemies. Underneath the novels I had put the Christmas postcards from my father. I stared for a long moment at my favorite. Two cowboys were on horseback, their rifles extended, pursuing a giant buffalo that was galloping for its life. Puffs of white smoke rose from the cowboys' rifles, but the buffalo continued to run toward freedom, unharmed, and the cowboys kept up the chase across the prairie, together. I liked it best because they were together. I always thought my father, when he chose it, had pictured the two of us like that, some day.

I put the false bottom back. I picked up the stack of paper, dipped my pen in the inkwell, and began:

Dear Becky,
I am going to Kansas to live with our father and I wish you would come with me.

Chapter 2

The sky was on fire in the west.

I remembered that line from one of my dime novels. I'd never seen a sky that looked anything like fire, until the evening I met my father for the first time I recalled. The whole western edge of sky, as I trudged down the train steps, glowed fierce orange. It took my breath away with pleasure.

And there he was at the station, his face like his photograph, only more faded. In the dim light I saw what the picture didn't show me: his eyes were brown like mine. He wasn't as tall as I expected. He wore a battered felt hat, a dusty, dark suit, and a white shirt, dusty as well.

I didn't know what to call him. His name was Joseph Hunter, but Mr. Hunter was too formal, Joseph too familiar, and I didn't know if he'd like Father or Papa, so I just said, "Hello, sir," and he didn't say different. He looked right at me, smiled, and said, "Hello, Thomas." We shook hands. He asked how my trip was, and where my things were, so we went to the baggage car where they unloaded my trunk. I helped him put it on the wagon.

I glanced about as we loaded, but there wasn't a town, only a hitching post the horses were tied to and a stock pen and the station, then nothing, stretching away after that—no trees, no hills. I felt naked, like anything protective around me was gone and all that was left was flat and shaggy grass, as if I could roll away in that wagon and no one would ever find me.

The town was behind the train. It appeared as we drove away, small wooden buildings, unpainted, only one street that I could make out. Then it disappeared, and I saw that the flat land wasn't flat, but a series of rises, one after the other, like waves on the ocean. It made me dizzy, this sudden nothing-then-something or something-then-nothing, depending on how you looked at it.

"We've a good three-hour trip ahead of us," my father said. Three hours from a train station. I hadn't expected the distance, wasn't sure how I'd handle the time with him. He talked a good deal on the way. He told me about the house, about my having to sleep in the big room with Caleb and Emma.

Caleb and Emma were my stepbrother and stepsister. I had read my father's letter over and over in Virginia, as I had gone over his picture, looking for clues in the rounded and pointed characters. He had mentioned my stepmother also, Mattie, and the baby, Jacob, who was my three-month-old half brother.

"Half brother?" I'd asked Grandfather.

"His son with his new wife."

Papa already had a son of his own living with him.

To be honest, I'd have to say that during the train ride I hadn't considered my stepfamily. I had pictured them, if at all, as waving at the door while my father and I rode off somewhere, to shoot buffalo or chase outlaws. Now, for the first time, I tried to imagine living with them. I liked the idea of being the oldest child, rather than the youngest. And the word *mother*, even if it had a *step* on it, sounded good to me. I was already forgiving them for living with my father a whole year before I had. If I was hurt because my father waited so long to send for me, I didn't admit it.

I hadn't thought of not having a bedroom. I hadn't thought about a house at all, only the prairie. But living in a log cabin sounded fine, like frontier life, like Daniel Boone. I pictured hunting game and cooking it over open fires.

We passed funny-looking houses that were made of dirt, with grass and flowers growing on their roofs. Sod houses, called soddies, my father told me. Farmers cut the bricks from the prairie soil with a plow and lifted them out, and the grass roots bound the dirt together tightly enough to hold a shape they could stack to form walls and roofs.

"Cool in summer and warm in winter, but hard as hell to keep clean, and they can fall apart in a good rainstorm. Ours is timber. It's the only timber house west of the creek," my father said. That was because it was one of the first, built when my father and mother bought land from the railroad in 1868. Those who came later found less timber for building and had to make do with sod.

My father's talking made me less lonesome. As the hours passed, I found myself just listening to his voice, not paying attention to what he was saying, letting the deep tones find a place in me. I paid attention, though, when he said, "Tomorrow we'll put you behind the plow. How are you at plowing?"

I didn't want to admit I'd never plowed. I said, "Plowing is fine with me," but I didn't mean it. I couldn't picture Buffalo Bill behind a plow.

The sky at nightfall seemed to open up and spill stars from one end to the other. The stars looked closer than in Virginia, maybe because I could see more of them, with no outline of a hill to block them. They swept down and touched the dark of the earth itself, in any direction I looked.

At first the house seemed like one of the stars, a light glinting brightly, distantly. But as we rode closer, I was flabbergasted to discover how low the house was—I'd thought it was the barn and kept waiting for the house to appear suddenly, as the town had. The house and a dark bump across from it, which my father told me was the barn, were the only buildings I could see in the dark.

The door opened, sending out another beam of light, and a woman stood outlined in the doorway, surrounded by the children. "I've got supper when you've put the team up," she called. She waved, then shut the door.

I helped my father unhitch, stable, and feed the horses. "What do they think of my coming?" I asked him. I was more nervous the closer we were to going in. I wanted them to like me, not to think me a greenhorn Easterner.

"You'll be fine," my father said.

The room we entered was small and firelit. Cupboards, crates, and beds crowded against the walls. A wooden churn stood in a corner and a bare plank table sat in the middle of the room, surrounded by four rough stools. I kept waiting to see the rest of the house until I realized that, except for a narrow bedroom at one end and an even smaller storeroom at the other, this *was* the house. We stood in what my father had called the big room.

The woman, Mattie, was standing over the cookstove in the far corner. Its fire provided the light. The children, Caleb and Emma, washed dishes at a basin perched on a crate next to the stove. Good smells drifted up from something frying. Mattie grabbed a tea towel to wrap around the pan handle and set it off the stove, on top of an upturned wooden box nearby, which held other pots and pans. The tea towel, I noticed, was really two sewn together. Both had holes, but together they covered each other.

"Jacob's asleep," she said to my father.

"I'm going to fetch him," my father said. Over Mattie's protest, he said, "Now, these two ought to know each other right off."

"I'll never get him back to sleep."

"All right. I won't wake him." My father disappeared into the bedroom.

"I've got mush for you," Mattie said to me. "No syrup. You hungry from such a long trip? I'm Mattie," and she stuck out her hand, but then withdrew it to wipe it on her apron, flushing.

We shook hands, and she pointed to the children washing dishes. "Caleb! Emma! Come say hello. Wipe your hands." They came forward, staring at me. They looked small for eight and nine, and stringy. The girl's dress was too short for her. Their hands and faces were scrubbed red. They stood together silently, without moving, as if they had been warned beforehand to behave and now weren't sure how to do it.

"Hello," I said, wondering what else to say. I put out my hand. They looked at it and then at their mother.

"Go on, shake hands, he won't bite," Mattie said. Caleb gave my hand a quick grip and backed away, but Emma was at first too timid, swinging her skirts and gazing at the floor. At last she touched my hand and retreated behind Mattie, who pushed her toward the unfinished dishes.

"They're not used to strangers," Mattie said.

My father reappeared with a motionless bundle, which he kissed as he held it. "This here's Jacob. He's noisier awake." My father beamed as he looked down at the baby.

I glanced at it. I didn't see what was so special. He looked like a regular baby. "He's very nice," I offered, mostly to please my father.

"Well, you two can get acquainted before long."

Mattie said to my father, "He can put his things under the bed there and then you two come eat."

The bed was a wide cot with iron legs, pushed into a corner behind a row of wooden boxes that served as cupboards for dishes. Carpentered cupboards hung on the wall next to the stove, and beneath them was a narrow wooden army cot. Boxes already filled the space under the iron bed. I shoved my trunk under as best I could, but it still jutted out about three inches.

My father stood a wooden box on end and pulled it up to the table for me. We all sat at the table as he and I ate. My father did most of what talking there was, asking about my journey. None of the others said much of anything. Tired as I was, I tried to oblige, describing the plush red velvet on the train seats and how I'd slept sitting up, and how the Mississippi seemed to flow directly under the train as we crossed it, as if we were flying over water.

I left out my shock at seeing the empty land, wanting them to think I was favorably impressed. I told them I'd never seen stars like I had tonight. The children were too shy to ask more about my trip. Mattie just nodded and said, "Oh yes, oh yes." She kept dishing out fried cornmeal mush for Papa and me. I was very hungry, but forced myself not to look around for the rest of the food, because I realized that this was all they had.

After supper Mattie cleared our plates and Papa showed me where to wash up outside and where to find the outhouse. He walked with me to the outdoor basin. "It's fine that you're here," he said, smiling and holding his gaze on me as if he didn't want to look away or I'd be gone. "Tomorrow I want you to see the farm. Tonight you must get to sleep. We get up early in this place."

When I came in, I sat down on the army cot and started to take off my boots. Emma and Caleb, in nightclothes now, ran to me, alarmed. "That's my bed," Emma said.

Caleb said, "You're going to sleep with me. Emma gets the cot, on account of she's a girl and it's warmer there."

I apologized to Emma and shifted to the bed, bumping my knee on my trunk. "This is a fine bed," I said, but in truth it was hardly wider than my single bed in Virginia, and I didn't see how the two of us would fit. I would have preferred the army cot, but it seemed right to give the warmer spot to Emma, even though on a May night like this, the house was airless and hot and the last thing I wanted to think about was more heat.

Already the arrangements in this home were complicated. To make it worse, the baby woke and cried, and I couldn't get to sleep even after he hushed. I lay awake for a long time, listening to the wind in the dark outside rushing through the grass.

Chapter 3

It was still dark when my father shook me awake. I thought there was something wrong, but it was just time to start chores. I had never done chores before, or any farmwork. My grandfather's colored hired man had done all that, although I took care of my own pony as far as grooming and saddling went. I stumbled over the horses' picket lines in the dark and couldn't get milk from a cow in the corral. My father said, "Hmph," watching me, and I could tell he was disappointed. "Lean against her side, like this," he said as he showed me how to pull on the teats, gently, rhythmically, one then the other. "Your grandfather's gone easy on you." I was surprised to hear him blame Grandfather, and mortified to disappoint him, but, try as I might, I got only a half bucket by the time my father and Caleb had finished milking all the rest.

Breakfast was the same as supper the night before, fried mush with no syrup, and just as quiet, except for the baby, who fussed through most of it. He undoubtedly got the most breakfast when Mattie, without any hesitation, unbuttoned her blouse and nursed him. I turned my head away, embarrassed. With her free hand, Mattie divided the mush, giving my father a big helping, but I got the same as Caleb and Emma. After breakfast my stomach still felt hollow.

My father led me out to the firebreak. "This is an important job I have for you, now. In dry weather, prairie fires are a danger. Eighty-one has been one of the driest years yet. Lightning can hit the grass and start a fire that can burn for miles, and good-bye to whatever stands in its way."

"Wouldn't the rain put it out, after the lightning?"

He stared at me, then laughed. "You're used to ordinary weather. Out here, rain don't always follow the lightning."

He had plowed two dirt furrows, overgrown now, around the house and barn, to keep the fire from reaching them. He wanted me to plow the break again.

Papa pointed out where he wanted me to plow. I had decided to call him Papa, but hadn't yet used the word to his face. He showed me which lines to pull to turn the horses and how far to push the steel blade into the sod. Then he left, and I was alone with the horses.

I had driven the buggy in Virginia, and figured this couldn't be much harder, but I had to loop the lines around my neck to use both hands for the plow. That worked as long as I plowed a straight line behind the barn, but when I had to turn to plow behind the house, I let go of one handle and the plow tipped. The horses kept going, the lines jerked my head forward, and my nose hit the plow handle. Blood gushed, but I didn't want my papa to see that I'd messed up so soon, so I sat in the grass and held a matted clod of dirt to my nose until the bleeding stopped.

In the dawn, the empty sky looked bigger than it had the night before, pale lavender, and the vast prairie, still in shadow, swallowed the light. I felt swallowed in the openness and wondered what I was in for. So far, except for the evening sky, the West was nothing like it was in my books.

To tell the truth, I never had believed all that was in those stories. But then again, on that shaggy prairie, I believed that anything could happen. It was like a huge, empty stage, waiting for an entrance. A herd of buffalo, galloping over the rise, maybe, or a band of Indians, sneaking silently toward us.

I stood up and went back to my plowing, turning my head as often as I could to scan the horizon.

I was able to finish the firebreak by noon, proud of making good time, but Papa, at a dinner of fried potatoes and bread, told me I had to plow another furrow eight feet beyond the first. We would burn the grass in between. That way, he said, a prairie fire couldn't jump it.

Papa barely paused between bites as he talked. The whole family ate noisily and fast off the crockery plates, and reached for food instead of passing. Seeing that the bread plate was empty and spotting a half loaf near the stove, I asked for more bread, but Mattie said, "I'm saving that for supper."

No one spoke then, and I looked down at my empty plate, not knowing what to do.

Finally, Papa chuckled. "You know, Thomas, I've seen crookeder furrows, but I can't remember when." The others joined in laughing. I blushed clear red at this. Evidently, I was supposed to ignore my hunger. I forced a smile at his teasing.

"I was watching for buffalo," I said. They started laughing again, and I was sure I blushed even redder.

"Only buffalo left around here are on the ground," Mattie said. "There's buffalo bones here and there. Watch that you don't blunt the plow hitting one."

"No live ones, not for six or seven years. Cattle, maybe," my father said. "Damn ranchers drive their cattle on the trails to Caldwell. Stampede now and again, right through my cornfield one year."

"There's a buffalo wallow," Caleb said, the first he'd spoken. He pronounced *wallow* as if it rhymed with *holler*.

"What's that?"

"It's where the buffalo used to roll in the dirt, years ago. Made a big old circle of dirt that you can still see. I'll show you, if you want."

"You've got to take the herd out again after dinner," Mattie said. "And Thomas has to finish his plowing. There'll be time to explore later."

But there was never time for "later." Everyone worked hard, all day long, and at night I was too tired to do anything but go to bed, cramped beside Caleb. Even the baby's cries and my blistered hands and aching muscles couldn't keep me awake.

Chapter 4

Trouble erupted soon enough. I thought my papa would run the household, but, after our morning chores, it was Mattie who gave each of us our day's work. During the first few weeks, as I fumbled through, she lost patience with me often.

In the barn one day, I raked piles of manure out of the straw, as the flies swarmed and the smell steamed, heavy and potent. I chased down a horse apple that rolled away from my rake, swearing under my breath at the amount of the stuff, too much for such a small barn. Pile after pile, and both of the horses were picketed out on the prairie during the day, in the barn only at night. They must have saved all their business for the barn.

My father kept the plow horses in the barn at night to protect them from the rustlers who plagued the country. They raided the outskirts of small farms in the night, he said, plundering nearly to Indian Territory by daylight. Rustlers meant adventure. I pictured a shadowy man, maybe even the outlaw Jesse James, galloping silently in the dark, the neck of his mount outstretched, a bandanna around his face. *He pulled his steed to a stop, jumped to the ground, and slashed the picket line of a terrified stallion, who reared and lunged. Swiftly the man leaped back upon his own mount, pulling the lines of the still-straining horse, who in its fright joined in the mad, midnight dash across the moonlit, open land. . . .*

"Jehoshaphat! I'm needing the fire for the baking and you're standing in the barn like an idiot, not even done sweeping out! Thomas! Do you hear what I'm saying to you?"

Mattie filled the doorway, skirts swirling and eyes snapping. "What do you think you're doing, dawdling in here? I'm needing the cow chips for the fire now, while there's some cool left to the morning. I've baking to do! You should have finished and spread the muck over the garden by now, and be gathering me those chips!" She grabbed the rake from my hands and I thought she would swing it at me, but she threw it on the straw and shoved me out the door. "I ask you! A boy standing around dreaming in the stink of the barn! Dump out the wheelbarrow now, you'll need it for the chips. You'll have to load all that dung back in it later. What were you thinking?"

I dumped the load I had stacked. I'd been up since before dawn to set the pickets for the horses, working with Caleb to water the stock and milk the cows before he took the herd to graze on the range, all before a breakfast that left me as hungry as when I'd started. "It doesn't matter what I do," I said. "You'd find fault with it."

Again I thought she'd strike me, and if she had I'd have struck back, but she stopped and said, "You watch yourself, and do as I say."

"I'm Papa's son, not yours."

"You can thank your stars for that. No son of mine could talk to me like that and sit the next day."

I stood watching her walk across the dirt yard to the house, its chinked logs weathered and dry in the light of the rising sun. Words I formed to yell at her retreating back died before I got them out. I couldn't satisfy Mattie. She must have hated me for being there, hated having another person to feed, one who took food from her own children. I thought of the hot, stinking horse manure I had to carry from the barn and spread around the vegetable plants. Her way of getting back at me. The flies would buzz and the heat and the smell would stifle me.

The trouble with the prairie was that there were few places to hide from my stepmother. Not behind the barn—that was the first place anyone looked. As far as I could see, there wasn't even a tree, except down by the creek, a stand of cottonwoods that wouldn't hide a rabbit. No houses, no road visible. Only rolling prairie wherever I looked, with swells that didn't swell high enough and waving short grass that wouldn't swallow me when I needed to disappear from Mattie.

I pushed the wooden wheelbarrow across the grass, which reached my knees once I passed the barn, and rippled in the hot wind blowing from the south. The grass was going to seed, and the feathery heads brushed against my pants, giving off a smell like baking. Viny sunflowers sprawled, their heads nodding up toward the sky, and the purple flowers on the scurfpea fluttered like tiny ladies' handkerchiefs.

About a quarter mile up a swell, the grass became shorter—cropped rangeland. The cattle herd, ten cows and their calves, would scatter over the open land, grazing during the day. My father earned most of what little money he had from raising crops, but he'd bought cattle after he married Mattie. They were Herefords, a breed new to Kansas, originally from England and expensive, with short, curly red coats and white faces. They were supposed to be good beef cattle and hardy enough to withstand prairie winters. Caleb and I milked them twice each day, Caleb hurrying to milk more than I did and then gloating. Mattie sold the milk and butter to farms that had no cattle of their own. The calves were for selling the next fall.

The cattle produced something else valuable in a country without trees: cow chips. The round, dried-out platters that the cattle dropped became the fuel for the woodstove, burning with surprising heat and little smell or smoke. Mattie swore they kindled better than wood and vowed to make her fortune one day shipping boxcar loads of the stuff back to the coal-sooted East.

But they burned fast, and I had to find a whole wheelbarrow load just to supply the baking fire. It was hot work, poking and prodding the dried-out platters loose from the grass, though the chips were everywhere and the dry ones didn't smell bad.

After I'd loaded the wheelbarrow I stretched out in the old buffalo wallow near the top of the swell, tired and discouraged. The wallow, ringed by violets that had dried and withered in the heat of summer, was a perfectly round bowl in the ground, about five feet across. When I lay full length in it, the rim blocked the house and the barn from sight, and I hoped blocked me from Mattie's sight as well. I pulled an arrowhead out of my pocket and held it up, silhouetted in the sun. I'd found it near bleached buffalo bones up on the rangeland. It was made from hard black rock—chert—the edges chipped by pounding until they formed a sharp edge and fine point. The bottom edge was notched to fit flat against the tip of an arrow shaft. Whoever made this knew what he was doing. I wondered what had happened to him, gone now, this worked stone the only sign he'd ever been here.

The heat wouldn't let me fall asleep. I got up and pushed the wheelbarrow back toward the house. The wind whispered through the grass as I walked, filling my ears with a sound like a note on a flute—one low note, unstopping. The dry grass crunched under my boots.

I reached with my rake to pull up another cow chip, and I heard a different noise, a rattling.

As I drew the chip back, I saw the snake coiled underneath. It arched its body and shook its tail in a rapid warning. I brought my rake down at it hard—in the dirt. The snake sprung and I dived, landing heavily on my shoulder. A swift movement parted the grass, but when I turned to look there was nothing. The snake was gone.

I sat in the grass rubbing my shoulder, breathing hard. The fear I hadn't had time for surged through me now. A rattlesnake.

In Virginia, there had been poisonous snakes—copperheads, water moccasins—but in all my explorations and make-believe games with my friends in the woods, I had never seen one. Dick Deadeye, in the dime novels I read, had shot rattlers many times. *He looked it in the eye, daring it to strike, and then, with a lightning motion, whipped out his six-gun and fired. The snake dropped dead, shot between the eyes.* Dick Deadeye would have come away with more than a sore shoulder. He would have carried the body of the dead snake home as a trophy. I had a sense of failing somehow.

Still, I hadn't been bitten, and I hadn't run.

I picked up the wheelbarrow handles, favoring my shoulder, and trudged toward the farm. About a mile away a rider suddenly appeared out of a prairie swell, his pinto pony galloping toward me, neck outstretched.

I drank in the flowing mane and the wide-brimmed cowboy hat, forgetting all about the snake. As he drew closer, I got self-conscious, aware of what I was wheeling. My life at that point was as far from his as if I were still in Virginia.

Horse and rider grew bigger as they neared, but not as big as they should have. The cowboy wore funny flapping pants that snapped like flags in a gale as they sped past.

"I'm training him!"

It was a girl's voice that yelled at me. I looked closer at the rider, now waving, and saw a mass of coppery hair pinned beneath the hat. The flapping pants were really a skirt tied up with rope.

She circled the galloping pony and tried to pull up as she sped past again, yelling, "Whoa!" But the pony barely slowed.

"For the drive!" she yelled as they galloped off.

Again they circled, and as they approached this time I grabbed for the bridle, but the pony veered sharply and took off across the prairie. The girl let loose some language that impressed even me, a veteran of schoolyard curses. I stood watching them disappear into a dot in the grass and then vanish.

I wondered what kind of place let girls run free like that. My sister, Becky, was good with a horse, but Grandfather never would have let her run wild, even if there had been open prairie to gallop across.

I wished I hadn't missed that bridle.

At noon, I told the family about the snake, but not the girl. I scarcely believed I'd really seen her and preferred to keep her to myself. My father swallowed forkful after forkful of potatoes as he listened to my story, and at the end said only, "Use a shovel when you're out gathering. It's heavier."

Mattie wiped baby Jacob's face with her hand and sniffed. "We're lucky to have this bread at all, you know, you took so long with the gathering. I barely had time to bake." And then she told on me. "Thomas, he didn't get his chores from the morning done."

"He was out lollygagging on the prairie," Emma added.

I scowled. Mattie glanced at my father, eyebrows raised.

She began reciting the afternoon's chores: Emma was to do the dishes, sweep the floor, and pick and snap beans from the garden. Caleb got to go with my father to help set barbed-wire fence posts for the cattle pasture. He stuck out his tongue at me as he heard this news.

And I, Mattie said, would take Caleb's place on the range with the cattle. "But he'll have to spread the muck on the garden yet first; and mind," she said to me, "you don't get Emma dirty when she comes to pick beans. If you'd spread it this morning, the plants would be having the good of it all the earlier in this heat and the dung would be drying so she could work in the garden without dirtying her feet."

I looked to my father for an appeal. All week I'd helped set fence posts. It was our only time together without Mattie, even though we never spoke much. And after the rattler I wasn't eager to go back out on the prairie. But my father only said, "You do as she says."

Emma cleared. My father pushed back from the table, patted Jacob on the head, took his hat off the peg, and motioned Caleb to follow him out.

I slumped in my chair, rebellion festering inside me. In the next room Mattie was putting the baby down for his nap, humming to him in hushed, soothing tones that came to me as if from far away. I saw the narrow room in my head, a gentle hand pulling the covers around me, brushing my forehead. My mother. She must have put me to sleep in that very room when I was small. I had no memory of my mother, just fleeting bits of feeling sometimes, like a carved chest opening briefly and shutting as I looked inside. The fight eased out of me. I got up from my chair and braved the heat to gather the dung.

Chapter 5

Papa drove the wagon to town one Friday to buy a new reaper blade for the wheat harvest. When he came back that evening, he had a package for me from Grandfather. I opened it after the evening chores. Inside the brown paper wrapper were three books and a letter from my grandparents. I guess Grandfather knew I wouldn't have packed the books if he'd given them to me before I left. Only one of the books, *The Odyssey* by Homer, looked even half-way interesting. Another, *Geography of the North American Continent*, sounded too boring to bother with. The third was bound in soft leather and had no title, and when I opened it I found that the pages were blank. A journal. I glanced at the letter. "Practice your writing in this," Grandfather had written. "I'll want to read it."

I groaned. I knew that he meant he wanted to read it when I came back to Virginia. Before I left, my grandparents had written my father, telling him to leave me where I was. They had argued with me night after night about going to the academy. But I knew that if I stayed, my life as far ahead as I could imagine would follow a pattern dull as the wagon ruts on the county roads. My grandparents had told me: Academy, college, a law office. Marry a nice girl from a good family and live there in the county forever, hemmed in by the Virginia hills. I would never know what was beyond them. Never know my father.

The only thing that persuaded my grandparents to let me go to Kansas was the assurance that I could come back. My father had promised them this, if things didn't work out, and I knew they counted on it.

So in my first letter to them I had tried to make my new life sound good and happy, and I saved my frustration for Becky. I had written to her: "There is never time to be with Papa, because there is much work, and I am not good at it. I am afraid they won't want me to stay. If you were here, it would be easier." I couldn't share these things with my grandparents. When I had to tell them there would be no teacher at the high school until January, I tried to sound sorry, although I wasn't. I didn't mention that Papa might not be able to spare me on the farm to send me to school, but I think they were worried and that was why Grandfather sent the books.

Mattie glanced at them while she ironed the wash that evening, after the heat of the day. "Your grandpa wants you to grow up studying, don't he?"

I frowned. "He wants me to be a lawyer, like he is."

Mattie laid the flat iron on the stove to reheat. She spoke very deliberately. "Way I was raised, wasn't time to waste putting your nose in a book. That's the way I'm raising the young ones around here." She folded her arms and stared straight at me, to see if I understood what she meant.

"I won't read when there are chores to do," I said. "I'll read afterwards."

"We can't waste oil in the lantern just so you can read at night," she said. "And when the sun's out, it is time to work." She lifted the iron and spat on the flat bottom. The spit sizzled against the hot surface.

It was peculiar how I reacted to Mattie. She told me not to do something I did not want to do anyway, and suddenly I wanted to do it. Those books and that journal became all at once highly desirable.

It wasn't just that she told me not to do it. The thought of not being allowed to read shook me. All the other adults in my life had forced me, had banned only the reading they didn't think fit. But I kept my anger in and just said, "Yes ma'am."

"It won't help you get ahead out here, just put you farther behind."

I glanced around the tiny cabin, thinking that they hadn't gotten ahead by *not* reading. She must have guessed my thought, for she stiffened and blushed. "I don't want to see you lazying around with those books," she said, and turned her back, pounding the iron against the table so hard it shook.

Papa came in just then. He must have sensed tension, for he raised his eyebrows at me, questioning and half angry. I help up my parcel. "From Grandfather. He wants me to keep up with my reading and writing." After all, Mattie wasn't my real mother. Papa was the authority here.

"And I say he needs to spend his time working instead of reading," Mattie said. "Hard work is what he has to learn around here."

Papa paused. "Write to your grandfather and thank him," he said. "But tell him there won't be time for study till winter, when the work eases." He thought a moment. "He won't understand why you have to work. Best explain that too."

Mattie looked triumphant. Why did my father have to take her side? I was worried—my grand-parents would make me come back if they knew I wasn't allowed to read. I didn't dare say this, though. If Mattie didn't want me here, this would be a reason to send me away.

I put the books in the trunk, slammed the lid. Caleb, in his nightshirt, crawled onto the bed. My father, holding Jacob, came over and sat down. "I wish it were easier," he said. "I respect learning. But there is too much work to be done to waste time."

"It's not a waste," I said, thinking how sur-prised Grandfather would be to hear me say that.

My father stood up. The skin over his cheeks tightened and his eyes narrowed. "Things are dif-ferent here," he said. He followed Mattie into the cramped bedroom.

Chapter 6

Wheat harvest was nearing, and worry worked itself into every corner of the house. Rain had been scarce since the spring wheat planting in April—none at all since I arrived. I knew, from the wheat fields in Virginia, that the green stalks should bunch thick and close like fur, not scatter thinly as they did. Mattie's voice had an edge to it as she woke us for chores. At breakfast my father stood in the doorway searching the sky for clouds that would mean rain. The air outside was still and close, hot and hard to breathe, but the sky was clear. "This crop will be good for nothing but barn straw," he said, and he spat into the dirt.

"Come eat your breakfast," Mattie told him.

I walked with him across the dry grass to the pasture where he was building the fence. He rammed an iron scraper down a hole to loosen the brown dirt, and I shoveled it out. We worked in silence as the sun rode up the sky, drenching both of us in sweat.

"Rest of the barbed wire will have to wait till fall," Papa said when he stopped to mop his face with his handkerchief.

On one side of pasture, thin strands of steel, studded with metal burrs, stretched for half a mile. To either side, for about a quarter mile each, catalpa posts stood in straight lines, naked against the prairie, waiting for the wire; and on the fourth side the open land stretched into the distance as if it were escaping. "Have to wait for the corn crop now to pay for more fence," he said. "I thought this would be the year. Don't get it so deep, now, it's going crooked."

I held a post while he tamped the dirt around it. "When do we sell the corn?"

"Not till fall."

I was glad the wire would have to wait. Fence on the prairie seemed a foolish effort to catch what shouldn't be caught, or to divide something that should stay whole.

We saw a line of cattle crawling along a prairie ridge about a mile to the west, driven by two cowboys on horseback. "Parsons' herd," Papa said. "Owns the two sections west of here. Thinks he owns it all, the way he lets them range. That's one reason we need this fence, keep his herd out of ours."

"It'd be easier to drive our cattle if we had horses like he does."

I had never seen a frown so deep as the one my father gave me, and I didn't know why.

"Cow ponies are expensive," he said, and he turned away as if I'd offended him.

We worked in silence after that. For a long while, I watched the cowboys work, listened to their yells, saw them gallop their brown horses after strays. They finally disappeared over the western rim of the prairie, leaving me alone with my father, digging in the dirt.

He noticed me staring at the cowboys. "I put you on your first horse, right after you learned to walk," he said, brushing the dark hair from his eyes, leaving a muddy smudge in the sweat on his forehead.

I was pleased, almost in spite of myself, that my father remembered my childhood. "I'm still good with a horse," I said.

"Now, how is it that you know so much about horses but can't get the barn mucked out in the mornings?" Papa was teasing, so I laughed, but at the same time I wondered if he felt the way Mattie did about my work. I wanted him on my side. "Yes sir," he said. "You sat up there on that big old horse, not afraid at all, like you were born to it. Right in front of the house. Right before your mama took sick." He paused, rested the sledgehammer in the dirt. "Your being here makes me think of things I ain't thought of for a while."

"I don't remember Mama. Just sometimes, I get a feeling, like something nice she might have done for me."

Papa nodded. "She did plenty of nice things." He stopped, frowned, then started again. "You ain't had a mother most of your life," he began.

"No sir."

"Well now."

He paused so long I thought that was all he had to say. I started to mention Mattie, to tell him how hard life was with her, but he picked up the sledgehammer again and swung. "These old posts can be stubborn to get to stand upright. Takes two people working with each other. If they don't work together, and the post goes crooked, it strains the whole fence," he said. He looked at me with one eyebrow raised, to see if I understood.

"Yes sir." I filled the dirt around the post, taking care to keep it straight. "I could work with you more. We could even drive the cattle when it's time to sell." I was leading up to a plan I'd been forming. Papa and I would go on our own cattle drive, just the two of us, with no one else to interfere.

Papa shook his head. That wasn't what he meant. "No . . . we won't sell them this year. The calves are too young. They need to be weaned at least."

I suppose I looked disappointed, because he nudged my shoulder and pointed to the distant riders. "Anyway, we're better off than those cowboys. They're just working to make Parsons rich." Papa swung another fence post into place. "This is all ours, and one of these days . . . "

He drifted off again, swung his sledgehammer, paused. "This ain't as bad as seventy-five, when the grasshoppers came, clouds of 'em. They ate everything, the wheat, the garden, the corn. Got into the well, the house. I lost all my crops that year. Had to go cowboy." Two deep furrows appeared between his brows. He spat again.

Had to go cowboy. My father had once been just what I wanted him to be. And he had favored risking everything on the farm, thought a cowboy was something to be ashamed of.

47

I held my hands steady on the post, trying not to show how I was spinning inside. I made my voice sound as everyday as you please. "Why did you quit?"

He grinned at me, his smile not erasing the lines on his forehead as he hammered the post into the dirt. "And give up all this fun?"

I promised myself I would make a note in my as-yet empty journal that next year was the time to sell the calves. I wanted to remember. Maybe I could wait that long to ride with my father. Maybe he could try to be a cowboy again.

As we walked back to the house for dinner, he grew silent. "About Mattie . . . ," he said. He stopped as we passed the wheat field and looked at the sky, distracted. There were a few wispy clouds, curved like sickle blades, low in the south-west. "Go back and get the tools," he said.

We had left them by the pile of fence posts. "But we're coming back after dinner," I said.

His voice hardened. "It's going to rain. Don't want them getting rusty."

I went back for the tools.

But it did not rain, that day or any of the follow-ing. The air thickened, day after day; low clouds built up in the southwest, lightning flashed, and then the sky cleared as if the promise of rain had never been.

And with each false hope my father's mood grew worse. He yelled if I didn't get the barn mucked out early, if Caleb spilled the milk pail or Emma dropped the egg basket. Mattie burned the bread and he even yelled at her, although she yelled right back. There was no more talk of memories or anything else as we put up fence posts. We just worked to get the job done. I wished for the rain not only to make the crop grow but to wash away Papa's foul temper as well.

Then rain came, near the end of June. At dawn one day the sky turned an anxious yellow, and the hot air pressed heavy on us as we sweated through our chores. "Clumsy fool!" I yelled at Caleb when he jostled my milk pail.

Midmorning, the temperature dropped, and the wind gusted a welcome chill on us, rippling the prairie and the wheat field. The sky darkened. Clouds piled up uneasy in the southwest, gray and purple, and then the wind pushed them in on us, with lightning forking among them.

Hard pelts of raindrops hit Papa and me as we stood by the fence, our faces lifted up to receive the moisture.

Then the clouds split, and cold rain lashed the ground in sheets. Lightning cracked the sky from top to bottom the same second that thunder deafened our ears as we raced home. We stabled the frantic horses, which had been thrashing on their pickets, then watched the rain from the shelter of the barn, feeling the shake of the thunder, smelling the freshness of the thirsty grass.

The dry soil couldn't soak up so much water, and miniature rivers snaked through the barnyard. Papa let the rain splash on his face, smiling, as if he would drink it in. I saw Mattie cross the threshold of the cabin and stand in the downpour till her hair and clothes clung against her.

The wheat headed out, unexpectedly. Over the next few weeks the sparse stalks, ripening into gold, gave off a heavy, nutlike scent.

Now, as we waited, we had a new worry, of fire and hail. Lightning could start prairie fires. And we no longer welcomed dark clouds in the southwest, especially if their bottom edges were green, because that meant a hailstorm. The clouds threatened but held off.

"This wheat won't be any good, but I ain't about to lose the little we have," Papa said. He made me plow a firebreak around the field. If hail came we couldn't do anything about it.

Papa and Mattie were still edgy as we waited for the wheat to ripen. Papa pounded his helplessness into the fence posts, and he did his chores like he was saying prayers, over and over like a ritual.

I didn't see how he could wait like this, a year's work at the mercy of the sky that he scanned. I was witnessing the daring that I had seen in my father's photograph in Virginia, but it wasn't the kind of daring I had imagined. He was like Odysseus in my book (which I read in the outhouse, the only privacy I had). Odysseus defied the gods, and he got knocked around plenty. And like Odysseus, all Papa ever wanted was to work in the dirt. I figured I was more like Achilles. He was a fighter, an adventurer, with a restless nature like mine. I wanted a future I could take command of.

Why would somebody choose the dirt over the cowboys?

Chapter 7

Caleb and I worked it so we traded off herding every other day. I loved wandering on the prairie, even if I was trailing after cattle. Summer wildflowers bloomed thick in the grass. I picked each kind and brought them home so that Papa could tell me the names at the end of the day. I wrote them all down in my journal, so I'd remember if I ever left: gayfeather, penstemon, leadplant, coneflower, Indian blanket. At the end of two weeks I had a hundred and forty-four names.

If Papa didn't know, I asked Mattie, who, I discovered, knew the name of every plant and animal anyone came across. She also told me, so I could write it down, that the rattler I'd fought was a prairie rattler, because of its broad brown blotches. Mattie didn't disapprove of my recording things in the journal, the way she disapproved of my reading. "Are you writing about us?" she asked.

"No."

"Well then."

I also sneaked books when I herded, hidden in my shirt. Legs crossed Indian-style in front of me, I read as much as I pleased as long as the cattle behaved, and no one was there to tell me to do different. At first I brought the dime novels I'd slipped into my trunk. They were thin and easy to hide. But after a few days of reading about the Wild West in those stories I got tired of them. They were imaginary, nothing like what happened in my West. All I had to do to see the real West was lift my eyes from the page.

I sat in the sun and read instead from *The Odyssey*, and when I grew tired I'd lie back on the grass and watch a red-tailed hawk circle or track the motion of the clouds across the sky, like long Greek warships crossing the sea. Then, when the sun was low, turning the grass and the shadows violet, I'd round up the cattle and head back to the farm. As long as I didn't stay too late and could see the sun, I never worried about getting lost.

One afternoon I saw the copper-haired girl again. She rode right up to me in her tied-up skirt, and the pinto pony stopped precisely.

"Hello, Thomas Hunter. I know your name and I know you're from Virginia. I'm Evie Parsons."

"What's E. V. stand for?"

She stared at me. "No, Evie. My real name's Evelyn, but my father says Eve-a-lynn, and he's English, and he likes things his own way. Evie is short for how he says my name."

The first time I met her I couldn't catch her horse. Now I'd embarrassed myself with her name.

"Is your papa the Parsons who owns the cattle around here?"

She nodded, then changed the subject. "You hunt? Your name's Hunter."

"Can't. I herd cattle every day."

"Well, I hunt." She showed me a pellet gun she carried behind her saddle. "For rabbits. And snakes."

I silently thanked my lucky stars she hadn't seen my episode with the rattler.

A bulging potato sack dragged behind her pony.

"Buffalo bones," she told me. "I get eight dollars a ton for them. And I get to keep the money to buy my own cow."

"Who would pay eight dollars for a ton of buffalo bones?" I asked, trying not to stare at the shine on her hair. Buffalo bones were so common I couldn't walk ten feet in some places without tripping over whitened, splintery piles.

"The railroad. They ship 'em back East, grind 'em up to sell for fertilizer."

"Why are there so many bones around anyway?"

"Buffalo hunters killed them for the skins. The factories back East made pulley belts for their machines from strips of buffalo hides. So the hunters shot the buffalo, skinned it, and left the meat to rot. Now all that's left is bones. But it's good money," she said, riding on.

"Maybe I'll see you again on the range," I yelled.

I asked Papa about her that night and he said, "She's a good girl, just born to the wrong family."

One evening, as I brought the cattle to the corral, three horsemen came riding over the prairie toward our farm. Papa emerged from the barn, and we watched the riders draw close and dismount. It was Mr. Parsons and two of his cowboys. Their horses were lathered.

I could scarcely keep from staring at the cowboys, with their silver spurs and exotic boots. One pair had the outline of a naked woman stenciled on each. I glanced at Mattie, who had joined us with the children, to see if she would shield them, but she didn't appear to notice.

Mr. Parsons didn't waste time on formalities. "The Weinhardts up near our ranch, they've run into some trouble at their place—their little girl has been lost since this afternoon. We're rounding up searchers to help find her."

Papa was already moving toward the barn. "Don't wait supper," he called to Mattie. "Thomas, you come."

Mr. Parsons told us more as Papa put the saddle on one of the plow horses. I had to ride the other horse bareback, which made me self-conscious in the presence of the cowboys' fancy black leather saddles. I listened as hard to Mr. Parsons' English accent, the first I'd heard, as I did to the story he told.

"The girl is just a snip of a thing, three years old, the same age as one of my own. Her mother took her to pay a call on the Mullers, three miles west. She played in the barn with the Muller children. Children will be children, won't they, and one of them told her a falsehood, that her mother had gone home without her. Well, the little one must have decided to walk home, because by the time her mother came to the barn for her, she was gone.

"They are meeting at the Muller place," Mr. Parsons shouted as he and the cowboys rode off.

Papa and I reached the Muller place before I realized we'd reached a place at all. About ten people, on foot and on horseback, milled around the base of a small rise in the prairie, and I wondered why they'd gathered there. Then I saw a wooden door and wood-framed window cut into the rise, and smoke coming from a stovepipe at the top of it. This was the Muller farmyard. A sod shed blended into the grass off to the side.

"I should have told you. The Mullers live in a dugout," my father said. He explained that the Mullers had lived there little more than a year, that they were saving up to build a real house with lumber imported from the East. Until then, they put up with living in a small cave dug out of the hillside.

Two men greeted my father in odd-sounding English. "Hullo, Jozuf. What a shame this is, eh?"

"Always worse when it's a little one. Any word?"

The men shook their heads.

"Fritz, Karl, this here's my son, Thomas, from Virginia."

Fritz and Karl nodded to me politely. "How you like this Kansas weather, Thomas? Too hot to spit, eh?" Fritz said. Karl just smiled.

"You get rain here lately?" Fritz asked my father.

"Not a drop. You?"

"No. We finish harvest, though, with that winter wheat. Not much bushels—ten to the acre. You plant the spring?"

My father nodded.

"When you going to start planting winter?"

My father shrugged. "I ain't convinced yet this country is best fit for wheat."

"What you mean? This is good wheat country, you see. Just plant the winter wheat."

"I ain't found a kind I like."

"The Mennonites up north, brought wheat from the old country that lives through winter better, they say."

"Is that so?"

"Don't know what they got this year. Course, if it don't rain, there ain't much you can do."

Fritz Graeber and Karl Schultz each had a farm nearby. They spoke to each other in a language clogged with consonant sounds—German, my father told me. This was the first time I'd heard a foreign language.

The Muller children ran around knots of people as if it were a holiday. I wondered which one, the girl or one of the boys, had told little Marie Weinhardt the lie about her mother, and how that one would feel if we never found her. None of them seemed particularly bothered right now.

Mrs. Schultz and Mrs. Graeber, speaking a soft flow of German between them, set rye bread and covered pots of food and coffee on a board balanced on chairs out in the yard. Mrs. Muller came out of the dark dugout to greet us. She spoke rapidly to the women in German, then told us, in English, where the others were out searching. "Mrs. Weinhardt, she can't stay here or at home, been out walking and walking, poor thing. I always worry it happen to one of mine. Who knows where she goes on that big prairie?"

"Why does everyone speak German?" I asked Papa when we were alone.

"The Mullers, the Weinhardts, and the others are part of a group of German immigrants that began buying land from the railroad nearly ten years ago. They just keep coming. Some of them haven't learned English yet. Many of them are

Alsatians who left because of political trouble at home. This group here is Methodist. The Catholics settled about fifteen miles east of here."

It puzzled me to think that the struggles of a country more than an ocean away could be felt here on the empty prairie.

I hadn't guessed so many people lived in the neighborhood. It was as if they had sprung from hiding places. Amazing that the prairie could hold all these folks and yet be large enough to still seem empty.

Papa and I rode side by side, searching east of the farm. Even though this wasn't how I'd pictured riding the prairie with my father, I was glad to be with him just the same. He and I rode straight, never moving out of sight of each other, calling for Marie and hearing only the wind. Only a few miles from the dugout, we were as alone as if we were the only two in the country.

"If you ever get lost out here on the prairie, sit down right where you are and let someone find you," Papa told me. Otherwise, he said, I might wander in circles and go crazy from the vastness that was all the same. There were few landmarks.

Twilight closed in and still we looked. Neither one of us, I guess, could bear going back without her. But the night was moonless and we had to give up: the dark became so thick we feared we'd get lost ourselves. We went back to the Mullers', hoping to hear good news, but the worried searchers had returned, lighting lanterns for a nighttime search.

Papa sent me over the next morning to help look for Marie. Mr. Weinhardt was sleeping on the ground by the dugout door, covered with a blanket. "He was out all night looking, he and some others, poor man," Mrs. Graeber told me. People spoke quietly in German around him. Even though I couldn't understand a word, I found I could guess what they said. They made gestures to the east, and I knew they were discussing where to search. They scanned the sky and I could tell they were guessing at the chances for rain, a concern in this place in any language.

Today, Evie was among the searchers, who, excepting her, were men. She wore her usual tied-up riding skirt. Her laugh was loud in the midst of the somberness, and when she ate she crammed the German potatoes into her mouth. I tried not to notice her, but she caught me sneaking glances, and smiled.

I stayed out on the plains that afternoon searching even when the heat and the sun were at their worst, thinking if the little Weinhardt girl had to endure it, I could too. I kept within sight of the creek bed, thinking she'd head for water, but also knowing I wouldn't get lost if I stayed near it.

In the late afternoon the sun began to cast slanting shadows on the rises, reshaping the land so that even the familiar creek looked strange. I rode about three hundred yards before I realized I was headed the wrong direction. Turning, I saw a movement in the buck brush along the creek, about a hundred yards south, so I hurried to check. The ground gave way to a shallow erosion draw, and in the draw I found Evie, taking a drink. Her pony stood quietly nearby.

Her funny tied-up riding gear had never looked so good. She eyed me, her head to one side.

"You're not lost yourself, are you? Sure we'll not be looking for you next?"

I scowled. "I'm all right. You don't have to worry about me."

"Who'd worry?"

"Thanks. I didn't know you cared."

She stooped to the creek and splashed water on her neck. "You got a knife?"

I did not.

"You best get one. If I ever got lost, I'd catch rabbits and skin them with mine. I wouldn't starve. Course, I'd never get lost. I tell you, I wouldn't want to be that child's mother right now. I hope she doesn't turn up dead."

I hadn't considered that I might be looking for a corpse. The shadows on the creek suddenly seemed sinister.

Evie said, "You have brothers or sisters back where you come from in Virginia?"

"A sister."

"Older or younger?"

"Older."

"You miss Virginia?"

"Some. I wanted to come out here, to be with my father. But it's not like I thought it'd be."

"What did you think it would be?"

I shrugged. "I don't know. More like your papa's cowboys, I guess."

She let out a hoot. "I pity you wanting to be like them. Dirty teeth and holey socks." She sat down on the grass, and I dismounted and sat beside her. My plow horse looked huge and clumsy beside her small cow pony.

"Cowboys are free. Not tied to a plow or a fence," I said.

She turned toward me. Her eyes were a peculiar shade of brown, like some sort of toffee-colored jewel. "I aim to ride with them, next cattle drive." She said this firmly, as if she expected me to object, so I didn't, although I didn't see how this was possible for a girl. "Your papa would let you?" I said.

"I'll talk him into it, don't you worry. I know more about cattle than my brother, and he went at my age. He's sickly, from pneumonia this winter, so he can't go. I'll take his place."

"When do they drive cattle, and where do they go?"

"To the railroad station at Caldwell, down south. They drive a herd this fall."

"Well, you've done a fine job with that pony." Finally I had the nerve to bring up our first meeting.

She laughed. "He behaves better than the first time you saw him, doesn't he? Still needs some work around the cattle, though." She stood up and dusted off. "Well, they'll be getting out lanterns soon. We best go back."

She rode close to me in the twilight on the way back to the Mullers'. We didn't say much, but I was glad of her nearness.

That evening it was harder to return, to face the red-rimmed eyes and ashen faces of Marie's parents and tell them I hadn't found her.

Chapter 8

"Couldn't Indians have taken Marie?" I asked Papa that night after I got home. We were all gathered in the yard outside the door to get the breeze, watching the stars and not yelling at one another.

"Doubt it." Papa looked up from oiling a harness he had borrowed, getting it ready to return. "There was Indians around now and then when we first come here. Story is some took a little girl up near Wichita, years ago. Her parents had to trade for her to get her back. But there's not many Indians around now." He settled back on his chair. "You heard about the Indian attack on town?"

I hadn't, of course. Neither had the others.

"I was livin' in town that summer, putting up store buildings. This was a year or so after your mama died and you children went back to Virginia. I didn't like living alone, and needed the money. Town was just getting started then, no more than a few families, no permanent houses, and we slept in the buildings we was putting up.

"It was one of those warm summer nights when you can't sleep. I just lay there on my blanket and listened to the katydids chirping on and on.

"Suddenly I heard hoofbeats on the trail that passed just outside the building. Someone yelled, 'Wake up! Come quick!'

"We ran out in our long underwear. It was Mr. Barker, from south of town. 'There's wagons comin' up the Chikaskia,' he said. 'People say the Indians are working north! Everyone's fleeing the country!'

"I must have looked skeptical, there in my underwear, because he turned to me and said, 'If you don't believe me, put your ear to the ground.' So I did, and sure enough, I could hear the clatter of wagons and hoofs miles away, coming up the trail.

"We got dressed faster than Jack Flash and grabbed our guns. Someone ran off to warn the people still living in tents and wagons at the edge of town.

"There we were. Many of the men had lived on the prairie a long time and weren't scared off so easy. We decided to make a stand, rather than run for it. The thought of being scalped sent chills down my spine, but I was ready to do whatever they told me.

"Teams came down the trail, galloping lickety-split. Women and children in the wagons were crying. We checked and rechecked our rifles. Tension ran high as we waited.

"And waited. And waited. The night dragged on.

"Someone made a joke about how we missed them when we blinked.

"Well, it began to get light, and we got braver. At dawn, we sort of laughed at ourselves for running outside in our underwear.

"No Indians ever did show up. Barker said he sort of wished they had, because any sort of excitement was welcome in those days."

"You forgot about the Cheyenne that escaped that reservation," Mattie said. "Two years ago. Killed and kidnapped their way across western Kansas."

Caleb and Emma, sitting on the doorstep, huddled closer to each other, their eyes wide.

"And the army killed pretty near all of them. The ones that are left are too starved to leave the reservation." Papa's face was sad.

"Good riddance, if you ask me," Mattie said.

"Why are they starving?" I asked.

"The Cheyenne pretty much lived by hunting buffalo," Papa said. "Now they're gone."

"They won't settle down and farm," Mattie said.

"Well, they get the worst land, and the worst food from the government," Papa said; "the maggoty stuff the army doesn't even want."

I had never thought of Indians before in any way except as they were in my dime novels, an enemy to fight with. Mattie thought of them that way, surely, because she feared them. I wondered at my father's sadness. If the Indians were still here, then he couldn't be, could he?

Then again, if he and other white settlers weren't here, the Indians wouldn't be starving on the reservation.

I went inside, and in the dimness pulled my trunk out from under my cot, and dug into a silk-lined pocket for the arrowhead I'd found on the rangeland. I'd drawn a picture of it in my journal and made a note of where I'd found it. The stone edges felt sharp under my fingers, could still pierce. I tried again to picture the person who'd made it. I saw him lash the arrowhead to its strong shaft, poise it on a taut bow, send it singing into the flank of a galloping buffalo. He'd take the meat home, to his family, roast it over a fire under the stars, maybe near where my family was sitting now. I hoped his family wasn't split like mine, a mix of people who belonged together almost by accident. And I didn't like to think of this person starving. The Indians had wanted to protect what was theirs, just as anyone else would.

And they'd lost it. To be honest, I was hoping they had taken Marie. It was easier to think that she was being looked after, even if a captive, than to think of her still out there alone.

Chapter 9

I heard hoofbeats while I was in the barn raking
early the next morning and came out to find Papa
talking with one of the Parsons' cowboys. The
cowboy rode away as I approached, flashing silver
in the dawn. Papa's face was sober.

"She's dead," he said. "No need to go over today."

He told me the story. Mr. Parsons had stayed
out searching by lantern late last evening, not
wanting to think of Marie out on the prairie
another night. He'd come upon an abandoned farm-
house, less than a mile from the Weinhardt place,
and knew a three-year-old would find such a place
likely, even though he knew searchers had been
there already. So he tried the door, but it was
locked, and the windows were boarded up. Then
something made him look under the porch steps,
and there she was, curled up like she was sleeping.
He spoke to her, hoping she'd wake up, but she

didn't. She likely died of exhaustion and dehydration, although there was a creek not half a mile from there. She could have seen her own house if she had gone to the top of the rise not three hundred feet away.

I didn't want to be alone that morning. I finished the chores early and hung around the house as Mattie got breakfast. Jacob fussed, and Mattie said, "Thomas, make yourself useful, will you, and mind the baby." I picked Jacob up and sat him on my lap. It was the first time I'd held him. I discovered I could make him laugh if I puckered my lips and made a *bpp bpp* noise. I watched him pulling at my shirt buttons. His eyes were brown, like my father's. Like mine.

It was a good breakfast, biscuits with honey from a hive in an ash tree along the Chikaskia River, where Mattie had gone the day before to gather sandplums. "I'll take honey and some plum butter over to the Weinhardts tomorrow," Mattie said.

She told Caleb to work with Papa, who was plowing sod. The thick tangle of roots held the dirt tightly clumped together even after the plow had turned it, so Caleb would have to follow behind with a long knife and break up the clumps.

"Let me do that," I said. "I can handle the knife better."

"Can not," Caleb said. "I can do just as good as you."

"That's enough," Papa said. "Thomas, you take the herd out east. Move 'em clear over by the Sweetwater today; the grass is getting all used up where they were."

"Caleb is big enough to take them that far," I said, trying an argument that both Caleb and Mattie might find appealing.

"Don't argue. You've been away for two days, it's time to get moving."

"Clean that plate first, Thomas," Mattie said. "I don't want a drop of that honey wasted."

All the other plates looked as if they had been polished. In fact, Emma was rubbing the last of her biscuit around on her plate, wiping up every smear of the honey. A few globs of honey and a tiny bit of a crust were left on my plate.

"That isn't enough to eat," I said.

"If you're wasting food, you won't be eating at all," Mattie retorted. "Then how would you like it?"

"You'd like it!" I cried. "You'd like it if I was gone. Then you could have my food, and Caleb could have my father!" I grabbed my hat and stormed out the door.

Out on the prairie with the herd, I picked up a rock and threw it as hard as I could into the empty blue sky. It hung, then plummeted down to the prairie with a dull thud. There was no danger of hitting anything, and no chance either. All that space. If I had ridden just a little way to the right or the left when I was looking for the girl, would I have found her in time? It didn't seem fair that her parents wanted her so much and she died, while mine barely wanted me at all, and yet here I was.

The prairie looked treacherous to me now, like the seas the Greek heroes crossed, and my book couldn't take the place of someone real to be with. I wished all day that Evie Parsons might suddenly appear as she had that once, but the prairie stayed empty except for the cattle. At least I had them. A herd of cattle wasn't good company, but they were living and breathing.

The lonesomeness didn't ease when I brought the herd in for the evening. I had filled my head with enchanted islands and magic sorceresses, but I couldn't tell anyone, because my reading had to be secret. The trouble of the morning was forgotten or ignored. Papa and Caleb had been plowing sod. They came in bone-weary but together. Caleb boasted of the acres they'd plowed. Emma showed me two pennies she'd earned from Mattie by plucking potato bugs off plants in the garden and squashing them between her thumb and forefinger, a penny for every hundred bugs collected in a tin can.

"I'm keeping them," she said with satisfaction, wrapping the coins carefully in a corner of her handkerchief. She had also minded Jacob as he played, while Mattie made plum butter and pickled and canned cucumbers, beets, and onions. The house smelled briny, and Mattie's face and arms were flushed red from boiling the jars of preserves. Marie Weinhardt was mentioned only once, when Papa said we would all go to the funeral.

The funeral was at dusk the next day, on a rise west of the Weinhardt place. The Weinhardts lived in a neat house made of new lumber, surrounded by neat fences and a large sod barn. The place looked industrious and more prosperous than most, but sadness hung over it thick as dust. Mr. and Mrs. Weinhardt were older than my papa and Mattie, and today they looked even older, their faces gray and their eyes wide. Their only other child, their grown son, Otto, who lived on his own farm, hovered near them, herding them from the house to wooden chairs set out on the prairie by the grave.

Men who had been searchers a few days ago lifted the small pine casket as they would lift a feather pillow and lowered it gently into the hole they'd dug. The Methodist preacher said a few words in German, and they sang a German hymn.

Papa and Mattie stood close to each other, Mattie holding Jacob. I looked for Evie Parsons, but only Mr. Parsons was there. The Muller children stood near their parents, red-eyed.

The men piled the dirt on the coffin until it was all buried. Marie's parents cried. Then it was over. She was left all alone on the prairie again, only this time her parents knew where to find her.

At home after supper, Mattie, in a rare mood, let Caleb and Emma play while we did the chores. Caleb hid somewhere outside and Emma ventured out to find him, calling, "All the wolves are gone," fearfully peering into the shadows cast by the house and barn. She would either find him or he would pounce on her, howling, and she'd shriek, and then she'd hide and he would brave the shadows and the threat of being devoured.

"Thomas, come play!" Emma called, and I joined them after my chores, but after five minutes I quit. The game was too childish.

That night Caleb took up too much of the bed. I pushed him, but he wouldn't scoot over. I pushed him clear off, and he hit the floor with a thud. Papa called from the next room to quiet down. Caleb didn't tattle, though. He crawled into bed and made room.

Chapter 10

In August it was time to cut, at last. In the field, the heads of the golden wheat stalks bent over with their scanty loads. Papa hauled out the reaper, a single-wheeled contraption with four rake arms sticking out like a windmill's, pulled by the two workhorses. A flat blade, bolted to gears under the iron seat, cut a five-foot swath of wheat stalks with a back-and-forth sawing motion. The stalks fell into a small bed behind as the arms, jerking down at a ninety-degree angle, swept them in and then swung up and around again. Every fourth sweep, a bar on the top of the rake arm opened the back of the bed and dropped a pile of the cut wheat onto the ground in an unruly pile.

Papa sat atop the iron seat like a lord, slapping the horses with the reins, glancing sideways at the raking and cutting, around and around the field. On the far side he looked like a puppet, and the reins like marionette strings, jerking him forward with the horses' steps, his black hat bobbing as the machine clattered, its arms waving against the sky.

Emma and Caleb and I, following behind, gathered the gavels, which were the piles the reaper dropped, and bound them into sheaves. We each took a fistful of long cut stalks, divided it in two, and tied the straw ends together in a square knot to make a binding, which we wrapped around the bundle, making sure the heads of wheat all lay in one direction. Then we tied and tucked the wheat-headed ends of the binding, one over, one under. Emma showed me how to do this, gathering and knotting with a deftness I didn't know an eight-year-old could have. "No, no. Look here, Thomas, bring this end *over* that one. And careful or you'll break the stalks and have to start all over."

I was considerably slower, fumbling the gavels and breaking the straw as I knotted.

We worked three days in the sun, ten hours a day, sweating under our hats, the dust settling on our necks and the straw scratching our forearms through our cotton sleeves as we bundled the gavels into sheaves and stacked the sheaves into cone-shaped shocks. I figured on my own how to build a shock tight enough to turn water if it rained again—which it didn't—and I was proud of the job I did, which was at least as good as Emma's.

Becky didn't answer my letter until the middle of August. Grandfather and Grandmother were well, she wrote, and Grandfather had bought a new colt to train for the buggy. "I hope by the time this letter reaches you, you are more comfortably settled and happier. It is a matter of making up your mind to adjust. But you'll always be welcome back home. We miss you."

Becky apologized for not writing sooner. After school was out she had spent a few weeks with her friend Ida Watson, at their farm near Norfolk, hunting for clams and boating along Chesapeake Bay with Ida's brother John. She had gone to parties around Norfolk and had met "ever so many interesting people."

I read Becky's letter lying in the dirt of the buffalo wallow, listening to the wind, out of sight of the house.

She wanted me to tell her about Papa, and especially about Mattie. What were her dresses like, and was she pretty?

How could I answer? Grandmother and Becky decked themselves out in lace, petticoats, and high collars. Mattie didn't wear any of that. I'd never seen her wear but two different dresses, neither of which could I describe, except that both looked dingy and worn.

I had to admit that when I arrived, I was very happy about Mattie's lack of fuss when it came to clothes. It extended to all of us—I never had to wear a tie or a collar. As long as what we wore was clean, it didn't matter.

But when I ripped my shirt on barbed wire, she said I couldn't have a new one. I had to keep wearing that shirt with a big mend down the front, she said, because throwing it out would be wasteful and cause more wear on my other shirts. Everyone's clothes had odd seams where they'd been mended or made over. I knew Becky would turn up her nose.

As for Mattie's appearance, I didn't think Becky would find her pretty. I didn't. *Durable* was the word for her. Her thick hair was once a chestnut color but was now more like iron. She wore it in a scraggly bun. Her face had been in the sun and wind a good deal and looked it, and her hands were large and rough. She was tall and carried herself very straight, like a lady, but her figure went slack where it should have been rounded and bulged where it should have been trim. She spoke too loudly and moved too forcefully to fit ladylike notions.

And no one in the family was particular about baths, except on Saturday nights. All in all, Mattie differed from the photograph of my mother in the silver frame as much as dust from water, and I didn't know what my father saw in her.

Becky's parties and outings had never interested me before, being as I was four years younger. But her letter now made me unbearably homesick—for music and laughter, buggy rides, even lace and china. For a moment, my grandparents' house was before me, not the prison it had once seemed, but a place of something gentle, where folks could rest and take their time.

"Grandfather and Grandmother send their love and hope you write soon," her letter ended.

I had chores to get back to. I rose, dusted off, and headed down the rise toward the cabin.

After the cut wheat dried, the hired threshers brought the threshing machine, red and square-bellied. We hitched our horses to poles that turned the grinders. Caleb drove the horses in a circle around the machine as we piled the sheaves in front of it like offerings. Papa and I cut the bindings and swung the bundled wheat stalks to the threshers, who stuffed them down the giant throat of the machine. It spit kernels of wheat out of a chute into the back of the wagon and spewed the chaff and straw into a pile on the ground.

We got the wheat threshed and bagged in good time—three days—without the catastrophes we'd been anxious to avoid. The real catastrophe was the number of bushels we got for the crop: only ten to the acre, at a dollar a bushel. I wrote this down in my journal the night before we hauled the wheat to town, not because I thought Grandfather would be interested, but because I wanted to know what kind of reward my father was getting for his efforts. Papa sat beside me at the table, mending a grain bag as I wrote.

"Papa, what were your costs for this crop?" I asked.

He was pleased I took an interest. "Seed was five dollars an acre," he said. "I didn't have any left from last year for seed wheat because we had to grind it all for flour. That's the main expense. Threshing costs eight cents a bushel, and when you include freight costs, you get about nine dollars an acre expense."

I copied all the figures into my journal and calculated. If we sold the wheat at a dollar a bushel, ten bushels to the acre, Papa made a profit, for all his work, of a dollar an acre. Papa had twenty acres of wheat, which meant a twenty-dollar profit. For the year.

"Is this what you get every year?" I asked.

"Hell no." He scowled. "This is a barn straw year. One year I made twenty-two bushels to the acre. It'll rain more next year. It'll be better."

Meanwhile, Caleb needed boots for winter and Emma needed shoes. We looked at them through the glass window at the dry goods store after we hauled the wheat to the train station the next day. But with so little money, and a mortgage on the plow, we left the boots and shoes where they were. Caleb and Emma and I daydreamed over the hard candies piled in wooden bins inside as the storekeeper packaged the necessaries for Mattie: flour, sugar, salt, salt pork, and coffee. "That'll have to do," Mattie said, frowning at our small bundles. I wanted to buy stamps and paper for writing to my grandparents and Becky, but Mattie turned on me. "We can't put shoes on the children's feet—you think we can buy you paper and stamps? So you can tell your friends back East how poor we are?"

84

That made me mad. I'd tried to hide their poverty from my grandparents. I turned away from her, caught my foot against the cracker barrel, stumbled, and knocked five jars of pickled eggs and pickled cucumbers to the floor, shattering every jar into glittering splinters that lay among the brine and the bulk of the pickles. Emma and Caleb stared at me, then at their parents. "Thomas did it," Emma said to Papa.

The shocked silence that followed unnerved me. I laughed, and I think that angered my father the most. He had never hit me, but he came close to it then. He leaned his head next to mine, his eyes like steel on a Winchester, and in a low, hard voice said, "Apologize." He made me clean up, and he asked the storekeeper how much he owed for damages. I couldn't believe he would pay for pickles and jars, especially when we had no money. The storekeeper wanted a dollar, but my father returned some of the sugar and coffee, and the storekeeper called it square.

"He works as hard for his living as we do for ours," my father said as we loaded the goods on the wagon. He was still angry with me. "You must never take advantage of someone else's hard work."

As we rode back to the farm that night, I felt as low as I ever had since I arrived. If this was the real Code of the West, they could have it. I hunched in a corner of the wagon and stared at the dark sky, thinking maybe I should go back. The stars, which glimmered back cold, spilled out in bewildering directions, every which way.

I overheard Papa apologizing to Mattie for the meager amount of money he'd made.

"You can't make it rain," she told him.

"There's the corn crop this fall. The butter and eggs, and the straw to sell. The cattle, next year."

"We'll manage," she said.

"Thomas." Papa's voice startled me. "I heard at the bank that the Judsons, east of us, are giving it up and going back to Ohio." He glanced at Mattie as he spoke. "This wheat crop finished them. It'll be open land, so that means we can graze cattle on their place. It's too far for Caleb. You'll have to do all the herding from now on. There'll be no fence before winter, that's sure."

At least he was still speaking to me. I didn't care to herd that far away, but I would prove to him, and to myself, that I could do the job. Maybe it was a blessing that I couldn't write to Virginia. That way I couldn't say I wanted to leave.

Chapter 11

Mattie found me sneaking *The Odyssey* into my shirt one morning as I dressed to go for the cattle. She didn't yell, but the alarm on her face worried me. "You can't be reading out there," she said. "If there's a snake, or if a cow strays, you have to go quick. We put a great deal of money into these cattle. Show your father he was right to trust you with them."

If my job was a matter of trust, it also seemed like a way to get rid of me during the day. "Nothing has happened," I told her. "I read only when the cattle lie down by the creek in the shade." This wasn't strictly true. I meant to read only when the cattle were resting, but many times I'd get absorbed in Odysseus' adventures, and when I'd next look up the cattle would have wandered far upland. I'd had to run to collect them.

She frowned, but all she said was, "I'll speak to your father."

Papa, as it happened, saw no harm in my reading. "He won't be able to go to school this fall," I heard him tell Mattie in their room that night.

"But what if he loses a cow?" she asked.

"He won't. He'd better not."

Mattie said something I couldn't catch, and then Papa said, "I can't see the harm."

I could hear Mattie's sigh. "It would be one less battle to fight," she said. Jacob stirred then and began to cough. "I'd best see to the baby."

I rolled over to sleep, smug with this victory.

Baby Jacob's cough deepened in the night to a rattling in his chest, so loud and persistent it woke us all. He coughed harder the next morning, a funny, strangled kind of cough that left him gasping for breath, and Mattie made Papa go to town for the doctor. Caleb dragged about his morning chores, saying he didn't feel well, and then Emma started coughing, so I hung around the farm instead of taking the cattle out, in case Mattie needed me. Mattie put the children to bed and ordered me to draw water, which she boiled all morning so that the steam would loosen the coughs. She barked at me to keep boiling the water and to offer cool drinks to the children, and then she went out on the prairie, carrying a spade. I stoked the fire, gave water to the children. Emma handed the cup back to me and said, "Am I going to die?"

"Of course not." Her directness startled me.

"Marie died."

"You are going to get well. The doctor will fix you up."

"How come you're not coughing? Don't people get sick where you come from?"

"No. Only the horses get sick," I teased. "Did you know I had a pony in Virginia? Old and slow as molasses. Ate some weeds that didn't agree with him one time and the only way he could get comfortable was to roll around on his belly." I pantomimed the way the horse rolled, making Emma and Caleb laugh, which started the coughing again.

"The poor horse," Emma said after the coughing stopped. "You shouldn't have let him get into those weeds."

"I guess not."

"Did you miss not having a mama and papa in Virginia?" Caleb asked.

"Some," I said. "But I have my grandparents."

"We don't have grandparents," Emma said. "We didn't even have a papa till your papa came along."

"Yes we did," Caleb said. "But we don't remember him."

"Did you remember your mama and papa before you came here?" Emma asked.

"No."

"Now Mama is your mama. But she was our mama first," she said.

"She'll always be your mama. I'm too big to need a mama."

Emma's eyes had closed, but now they opened in surprise. "Everyone needs a mama," she said.

She fell asleep then. Jacob whimpered, and I rocked him. He was awfully listless.

Mattie returned, carrying a cluster of cleaned roots that she chopped and steeped in hot water to make a tea, which she forced all three children to drink.

When the doctor came, the children were sleeping. He examined each one, asked me if I'd ever had whooping cough. I said no. The doctor gave Mattie some brown syrups, said the children's breathing didn't alarm him, told her what to do for the coughs, and left.

By the evening, all three children were coughing again, and Mattie dosed them with the syrups and told me to brew more tea. "Snakeroot," she said, when I asked her what it was. "Old Indian remedy."

"I thought you hated Indians."

An odd expression crossed her face. "I'm part Shawnee. Not the kind that murders folks on the prairie." She kept talking as she stooped to give the children their syrup. "My people were traders on the Santa Fe Trail, way back fifty years ago. My grandfather married with the Shawnee, my grandmother was from an important family in the tribe, went to the mission school. Grandpap was rich. He crossed this country a hundred times." She straightened and turned toward me. "I know this country, I lived here all my life, not like most. That's why if I say something should be done a certain way, there's a reason for it." Her face was weary and anxious, her forehead lined, her hair falling from its knot in the back. She wasn't old, I realized with a shock. She wasn't yet thirty. "This place can be harsh, if you don't watch out," she warned.

By the next morning, Caleb was sitting up and eating. The coughing had left Emma and Jacob. Papa and I left to work in the cornfield.

But in the afternoon, Mattie came racing to the field, crying. "Get the doctor! Oh, my baby!"

Papa hurried to her, and together they dashed to the house. I followed. "He gave a shudder, and that was all," I heard Mattie wail as I ran in.

Baby Jacob lay in his bed, eyes open but not moving. Papa was saying, "The doctor can't help us now."

Mattie was lying across the little bed, her arms around Jacob. "I can't close his eyes," she sobbed. Caleb and Emma crawled out of bed and stood by me, their faces frightened. "Is he dead?" Caleb whispered. I nodded, and put my arms around both of them. My father's face contracted, tears sat in his eyes, and his lips fixed together, hard and purposeful. He reached out and laid a gentle hand on the baby's eyelids, closing them. Now Jacob looked like he was asleep.

We buried Jacob on a rise past the garden, where Mattie could watch over him when she worked. The preacher came out from the German settlement to say the funeral, in English this time, and the German families brought food. Mrs. Weinhardt gave Mattie a long hug.

The days after Jacob's death went by as if we were sleepwalking through them. Caleb and Emma got well, but the whooping cough left them too weak to help with the work. I was glad for the chores that kept me around the house, but I thought I should feel sadder. I had felt more sadness when the Weinhardt girl, a stranger, died. Jacob was a blood relation—half, anyway—and all I felt was distance, and relief that I hadn't taken sick in this place.

Mattie was like someone after a hard drunk. At first she slept most of every day. Then, after a week or so, she would crawl out of bed and sit in the doorway in her nightgown, staring across the grassy space to the cross out there by itself on the prairie.

"She's never lost anyone before," Papa told me as we washed the clothes and spread them on the grass to dry. We had burned the children's bed-sheets and nightshirts a few days before. "She was a grass widow when I met her. That first husband of hers, he run off. She likes folks to think he died; most don't know. He's probably dead by now anyway, but she never cried for him."

He kept working, as if what he'd just said was matter-of-fact. I stopped trying to untangle a skirt and stared at him. Here a startling piece of Mattie's story. How could my own papa have married someone who was already married? Papa's phrase, *It's different out here*, apparently applied to everything. I thought of how my grandparents in Virginia would react. The news would set their carefully balanced world on end.

"She was dead poor when I met her, doing laundry down in Caldwell for the cowboys from the trails to feed herself and the children. I felt sorry for her, and I admired her spunk. She could have done a lot worse. She never wanted folks to think she wasn't respectable. So we never let on she wasn't legally unmarried."

As he spoke he scrubbed a shirt against the washboard again and again, although the dirt had already washed out. "Work's the best medicine for trouble," he said, almost to himself. "Just keep working, get through it."

That was his way. I never saw any more tears or signs of sadness. I wondered if work had saved him when my mother died, if he had plowed his grief into the furrows, swung at it with his hoe to keep it from overwhelming him. Was grief the reason he'd sent Becky and me to Virginia? Had it allowed him to bend the rules with Mattie?

But he was right about the work. Mattie began to dress herself in the mornings and get meals again. She became, by turns, distant and snappish, but there were chores that pulled her to them, and she sank into them as one sinks into a lifeboat.

The corn didn't need much weeding now, so Papa said Caleb could go with me to herd. I took old potato sacks with me, determined to try bone collecting.

Some days I came home with a full sack, but just as many I arrived with it empty. The bleached buffalo bones weren't hard to spot, lying bleak and ghostly on the grass, but they were scarcer than I'd thought. I prized the skulls for their weight, and kept track of their number in my journal: nine so far. I drew a picture of a buffalo skull beside my record. The bones themselves I piled behind the barn, where they began to form an eerie white mountain. Papa said we'd haul them to town in the winter, once the farmwork eased.

Caleb and I hunted silently, even when we walked together. We must have looked like ghosts ourselves, drifting over the grass. Dried stalks of wild indigo stuck up from the short grass, dancing like skeletons in the wind.

One afternoon, when my sack was full, I motioned to Caleb to head back toward the herd. But Caleb, a quarter mile away, kept walking, disappearing behind a swell of land.

I sat down and waited. Nearly half an hour passed before I spotted him, dragging his sack with great effort. "I found a skull!" he yelled, and his voice startled the cattle. They jerked their heads up sharply and watched him without turning, poised. Then they lost interest and nosed at the grass.

Buffalo skulls were hard to find. I ran my fingers over the flat, cracking skull and the smooth, almost polished curve of the horns. "He must have been a giant," I said.

"Yeah," Caleb said with satisfaction. "With that skull in it, bet my sack's heavier'n yours."

"Bet so. You do a man's job, hauling that sack."

"I can plow too, next year. Bet I can plow more than you."

I looked at the boy, small for his age. His face was dirty and his sand-colored hair stuck out at uncertain angles. "Why do you always want to do more than me?" I asked.

"I don't know." Caleb shrugged. "Bet I can be as good as you, though." He too ran his fingers along the dry surface of the skull and stared at the empty eye sockets and hollow nose. "Thomas, do people get like this when they die?"

"I guess so."

Caleb kept looking at the skull. "Is Jacob like this?"

I shuddered at the unexpected question. "Jacob's in heaven," I said. "But, well, it's like this. The part of him that was earth, it goes back." Dust to dust, the Bible said.

Caleb considered this. "He ate some dirt one time, but that was the only earth in him. The rest of him was the same as you and me."

"No, not like that." I had never thought about it before, and now I explained it as much to myself as to Caleb. "We're part of the earth. Our bodies need food that grows from it, and they need air and sun and water—that's all part of the earth. When we die, our bodies go back to it and our spirits go to heaven."

"Did the buffalo spirits go to heaven?"

I had to think awhile about that one. "Sometimes, when I hear the wind blowing and watch the grass waving, I think their spirits are still here."

"Still here." Caleb leaned his hand against my shoulder, scrutinizing the prairie. "I made Jacob eat that dirt," he said after a time. "I wish I hadn't."

I put my arm around Caleb. "He probably didn't mind."

Caleb smiled. "He liked it. He smeared it all over his mouth. Mama had to wash him off." He twisted away and contemplated my face. "You and me are the only brothers now."

"Looks that way," I said.

Chapter 12

One morning, out herding on my own, I couldn't get the herd up on the range. They stayed down in a shallow draw that in the spring was the Sweetwater Creek but which was now a rutted, dusty path through the grass, lined with straggly cottonwoods, about two miles south of the farm. Well, the cattle were fooling themselves if they thought they could find water in that draw. I didn't know why else they would be down there.

I had noticed that the best grass, this time of year anyway, was up on the swells, where the blue-gray grass stems held something they liked, and every time I herded them into the bottomlands they ended up on the tops of the rises that Mattie called hills, which back in Virginia wouldn't even be noticed. Only in the day's worst heat would they come down to the scarce shade of the trees.

Now, in the middle of the morning, the cattle wouldn't go upland for anything.

I gave up trying and threw a rock down the creek bed, away from the herd. I'd made a game of throwing for distance. I would stand in front of one of the cottonwoods and throw as far as I could, gauging by the trees. Then I'd try to beat the distance with my next throw.

The rock landed with a puff of dust among the weeds, farther than I'd expected. I spanned the girth of my upper arm with my thumb and finger and was pleased at the size, bigger than when I'd arrived.

"Fighting off the wolves?"

I spun around. There was Evie on her pinto pony, riding up the creek bed. I hadn't heard her coming, I'd been so absorbed in my game.

"Well, you never know. If any hungry wolves come around to devour these lazy beasts, I'm ready."

"They say there are wolves on the Ninnescah River now, you know."

"There aren't any wolves in Kansas." I'd ask Mattie, to be sure.

She shrugged. "It was in the newspaper the other day. A pack of 'em. Got some cattle. You'd better watch out."

"Aw, wolves aren't going to bother me. I'm ready for them."

She eyed me. "Bet I can throw farther than you."

"You prepared to make good on that bet?"

She dismounted, and for the next hour we threw rocks and ran races. She could throw pretty far and run pretty fast, I had to give her that.

We sat down to rest, and she noticed my empty bone sack. "You ever have any luck selling bones?"

"I've got nearly a ton by now. We'll sell them this winter." I didn't know if I had nearly a ton or not, but I figured it was possible.

"Well, I bought a cow with my bone money. A Durham, one year old. She grazes on the range with the rest of 'em, though, so I never see her."

She plucked a blade of grass, folded it, and blew on one end to make a noise. The grass was too dry, though, and broke off.

"I heard your little brother died," she said.

"Yes. Whooping cough."

"Did you get sick?"

"No. Caleb and Emma did, though."

"We didn't come to the funeral because my big brother is sick."

"What's wrong with your brother?"

"Pneumonia. Again."

I pulled at a weed in the dirt. "I don't miss Jacob that much," I confessed to her. "I feel like I ought to, but I don't."

"Maybe you didn't know him all that well. I worry about my brother dying. He gets sick a lot. I never do. He couldn't take the cattle to market again this year." She paused. "I couldn't go either."

"That's too bad."

"Well, one of these days." She stood up and brushed off her skirt. "I'd better get home for noon dinner."

The prairie was extra empty after she rode out of sight. I ate my own dinner by myself. I threw some more rocks, but that made me think of wolves, so I stopped.

The cattle began to low in soft, answering voices that became louder and more urgent. I ran down the draw. The cows had bunched together, and their big calves huddled close to them, bawling. They began to mill, swinging their heads. I scanned the prairie for coyotes, snakes, anything that might frighten the cattle, but saw nothing alarming. Tornadoes sometimes swept the prairie without warning, I'd heard, but the sky was clear and sunny.

I wished I had more than my snake stick with me. Buffalo Bill would never have come out alone on the prairie without his rifle.

I saw a long brown cloud now rolling on the rim of the prairie to the south, maybe two miles distant. Was it fire?

The herd grew more agitated. A few of the cows trotted straight for the dark bulk, lowing. I ran after them, tried to turn them toward home, where the firebreaks were, but they wouldn't turn. They veered away from me as I ran at them, waving my stick. Then they swung back, toward the angry cloud, which headed straight at us.

Not for the first time I wished I had a horse and a dog to help me, like the cowboys did.

I picked up another rock and threw it just ahead of the cows, hoping it would startle them into the right direction. The rock landed closer than I'd intended. It spooked a cow, who bawled and ran.

The herd, alarmed, took off as one body toward the threatening mass, which rumbled closer in the distance.

I ran after them, yelled, waved my arms, but I couldn't catch up. Figures moved at the bottom of the turmoil now, other cattle, pounding toward my herd. Over the rumble I heard frightened bawling, saw men on horseback galloping with them, waving their hats. I heard their sharp whistles and cries as they tried to control the herd.

My herd scattered before the oncoming stampede. Stretching far back into the dust, a mass of brown backs and long, pointed horns headed right at me. The stampede gained on us; it would soon overtake my herd, and me with it.

Chapter 13

The dust rolled in from every side, choking me. Papa's cattle dissolved into the stampede, the calves bawling for their mothers. I hurled a rock at the mass closing in on me, yelled and waved my arms. Not fifty feet away from me a longhorn at the front stumbled and was swept under the pounding hooves.

I ran as fast as I could back toward the dry creek bed and the thin barrier of cottonwoods, away from the crashing torrent headed now upland. The edge of the herd blurred past in a tangle of dust and noise. A cowboy on his horse flashed between me and the press of the cattle, turning the nearest one away from me. I ran on, until the sharp horns were several hundred feet away and I began to breathe through the dust. My lungs ached for air. I pulled my handkerchief from my pocket and tied it so that it covered my nose and mouth, like the cowboy bandannas, blocking the choking dirt.

Cowboys pounded past in the wrong direction. One galloped across the front of the herd: if his horse had stumbled, he would have been crushed in an instant under the hooves; but the cattle instead veered away. The cowboys were trying to turn the herd in a circle, to stop the stampede.

It didn't work. As soon as the front started to turn, a stray would bolt and throw the whole herd into roaring confusion.

The cattle thundered into the distance. I yelled curses after them, as many as I remembered from the schoolyard in Virginia. Then I dropped beside the creek bed, exhausted from fear, wondering how far the longhorns would run. I lay there and waited until my heart stopped thundering as well.

What had I ought to do? I hadn't recognized the cowboys or the cattle—busy escaping the crush of the hooves, I didn't notice details. They probably weren't local. Some of the ranchers around had longhorns, but most kept Angus or Durhams.

Whoever they were, I decided I had to follow their trail and bring my cattle back. Papa needed them, and I didn't want to let him down.

For the rest of the afternoon I followed the stampede, never gaining on it. The trail was easy to follow, trampled grass a hundred yards wide, and a cloud of dust in the distance. I came upon a cow that had fallen. Its back leg stuck out and twisted up, and blood ran from a hole in its temple—shot to end its suffering. Flies swarmed around the blood. I found other carcasses, some shot, one pounded into a dirty, bloodied hide with twisted horns. A live stray grazed a quarter mile off. It raised its head, and even from that distance bolted across the prairie as I took a step.

Toward sunset I lost the cloud of dust altogether, but I kept following the wide trail. I could not recover the herd before nightfall. I thought about turning back to the farm, but didn't want to face Mattie's ridicule and my father's disappointment. My boots hurt my feet, and my legs ached. The sun turned the sky and the land pink, then violet, then gray as it glowed full red at the edge of the prairie and sank below the rim. The evening star appeared above it in the smoky blue of the night sky. The land was shadowy and still. A horned owl hooted from its burrow far away.

For a time after sundown, I used the evening star as a guide, but as other stars began to crowd the sky, it swam and ducked among them, and I was no longer sure which way I headed. More than anything, I did not want to be lost on the prairie. I shivered, though the night was warm. Remembering my papa's advice, I sat down where I was to rest for the night. I was thirsty, but didn't dare search for a creek or stream to drink from. Stars scattered thickly over the black sky like numberless wandering campfires.

Then I heard music. It was high pitched, like a coyote yowl, and my skin prickled, but it kept going in a melody, thin and reedy, and I ran to the top of a low ridge that dropped away into a broad, sloping plain below. A glimmer about a mile away, too low for a star, drew my notice. It might have been a campfire. I headed toward it.

As I drew closer I saw the cowboys, five of them. They stretched on canvas and striped blankets, squatted by the embers, or lay propped against saddles in the grass near the fire. Their faces, under their hats, were red and shadowed in the firelight, still as wood carvings. Beyond the firelight in the dimness, their horses, on picket lines, grazed calmly, and farther back, in the dark, music-makers sang to the cattle as they rode the edges of the herd to quiet it.

> *A cowboy's life is a dreary, dreary life*
> *Some say it's free from care*
> *Rounding up the cattle from morning till night*
> *In the middle of the prairie so bare*

I didn't say anything as I walked to the fire—I didn't want to scare the cattle or break the cowboys' silence, afraid that if I spoke they would disappear. The song was the only sound—the herd was quiet. I could see it outside the firelight, spread out, a black shape against the darkness.

When the cowboys noticed me, they scarcely moved.

"You lost?" one asked.

"I've followed you." *What do you say to a cowboy?* I wondered. My tongue felt thick and dry from thirst and from not talking. "You have my cows. They ran off in the stampede."

"Damn!" A tall cowboy in a brown felt hat sat up and spat. "Ain't you scared to follow us into the dark?"

It hadn't occurred to me that these might be rustlers. My stomach clutched.

Another cowboy, his hair matted down from where his hat had been, stood up from where he'd sat leaning against his saddle. He brushed the dust and grass off his pants and shook my hand. "Don't let Mick worry you none. You're the boy we saw this afternoon, 'bout got trampled."

I nodded.

"You must want these animals pretty bad, boy, to follow us at night. We'll cut them out for you in the morning, sure thing. Luke Fitzgerald," he said.

"Thomas Hunter."

"These characters here are Shorty, Mick, Lightnin' Jack, and Oscar. We got Ben and James back with the herd." The cowboys nodded at me as Luke said their names, but they didn't speak.

"Better pull up some grass there, Thomas, and rest for the night. We chased these damned animals for miles today and we don't want them starting up again, so excuse our manners if we don't visit with you. Got no food to offer, our chuck wagon's back toward Caldwell, wondering where the hell we are."

He nodded to me and lay down. His bed for the night was a wool blanket stretched on a canvas square on the ground, with a cloth sack full of his belongings for a pillow. He took off his

boots, grunting and tugging, and stuck them behind the sack. He pulled the top side of the canvas over his sack and boots, folded the edges of
the blanket and canvas around him so that he was
wrapped like sausage in a casing, ready for rain if
it came, and propped his hat over his face. The
other cowboys did the same.

I found a level place in the grass to stretch out.
I was easy in my mind now. These weren't rustlers.
I knew from Papa that Caldwell was a stop on one
of the cattle trails from Texas I'd read about, the
Chisholm Trail. Tired as I was, I had a hard time
falling asleep. I couldn't stop watching the cowboys. The firelight flickered over their saddles,
touching the black leather and polished wood with
light. It shadowed their lariats hanging in loose
coils from the saddle horns and glinted off the
gaudy silver spurs on the boots that stuck out of
the bedding. Finally I drifted off, the music of the
cowboys blending with the music of the wind in
the grass.

Chapter 14

"Up, boy, up. Time for lazin' is past."

Long before dawn, Lightnin' Jack, wearing an old Union army hat, kicked at the soles of my feet. "Up you go. Danged longhorns are still feisty," he grumbled. "Musta run miles off the trail yesterday. Rabbit spooked the front, near as we can tell. They run all day, stopping and starting. This ain't nothing, though, compared to a herd I was with in Texas, run for three days and three nights without stopping. Wasn't nothing to do but let 'em run."

I pulled myself off the ground. My muscles were stiff from the hard bed, but I tried not to show it.

Luke took me to the remuda, a group of spare horses the cowboys kept, hobbled with rope tied around the forelegs, so the horses could graze but not wander off. Luke's blunted spurs jangled when he walked, and the brim of his black hat was turned up above his face. He carried his bridle, saddle, and horse blanket over his shoulder. "Your folks'll be worried about you," he said as we walked. "Why'd you chase them cattle all the way out here?"

"My folks can't afford to lose the herd," I said. "I don't think they'll miss me as much as the cattle, anyhow."

"Don't get along with your folks?"

"I have a stepmother, and we don't get along."

We came to the horses. The other cowboys were already there, quietly saddling their fresh mounts. Luke swung the horse blanket and saddle with ease onto his horse's back.

"I'll fetch my other horse for you off his picket. Today's supposed to be his day of rest, after yesterday, but don't count on that making him any easier. That's one ornery horse, I'll warn you."

He slipped the bridle over the horse's head and eased the bit into its mouth, then took the hobble from the horse's forelegs. The dawn was still, but already the cattle stirred.

"What happened to your horse, boy?" Luke asked, pulling on leather gloves stitched at the top with red wildflowers.

"Don't have one," I said. "My papa needs the horses for plowing."

"Plowing!" He snorted, and I felt a quick flush of shame.

"You even ride?" he asked.

"Yes sir. Back home in Virginia I rode."

"Virginia boy, are you? Shorty over there's from Virginia. He was a slave till he was ten years old. Came west after the war ended. Best roper on the place."

A small colored man in a leather vest and red scarf sat a few yards from us, retying the knot on his lariat. I hid my surprise. I hadn't known there were colored cowboys.

"You ever roped?" Luke asked.

"No sir."

"You're goin' to need to rope." Luke pulled his rope from his saddle horn and showed me how to tie it so it made a loop with a sliding knot. "There's your lasso," he said. I liked his word, *lasso*. Better than *lariat*, a dime novel word. He tossed the lasso, sweeping his arm up and out, palm down. "Just dangle it there in front of you, then give 'er a toss as you ride by slow, and pull."

Luke rode off to collect a horse for me.

Meanwhile, I practiced with the lasso. I swung the loop and then tossed it at a brown saddle with a wooden seat and horn about fifteen feet away. I missed the saddle horn and dragged the rope back across the grass. I thought of Dick Deadeye, riding at full gallop and yelling a wild whoop as he twirled the lariat high over his head. But if I rode for the cattle at a full gallop, I would scare them off and make my job harder. And tossing the rope the way the cowboy showed me meant less chance of tangling it.

"Ain't no chance of that saddle gettin' away from you, now. You leave it be, hear?"

Shorty was walking toward me, a worried look on his face. His legs bowed, and he was shorter than I had first thought, no taller than I, although the high crown of his hat made him seem taller. His high-heeled leather boots were embroidered at the tops with stars. "Take all the rest, but don't touch the saddle. That's my livin'."

He took the rope and examined the knot I had made for the lasso. "Not bad, young man, for the first time. Look here, now."

With a swift motion he swung the lasso up and out, roping a branch of a bending young cottonwood twenty feet away. "Just easy, like that. Now you try," he said.

I tossed the lasso at the tree, moving my arm up and out as Shorty had, and this time I caught it.

It tangled on a branch, so the knot didn't slide to close the loop like it was supposed to, but I was proud just the same.

"That's right," Shorty said.

"Luke said you're from Virginia. Me too," I told him as we untangled the rope from the tree branch.

"That's one place I don't care none to go back to," he said.

"Me either. How'd you get to be a cowboy?"

He looked at me as if he wondered what I really meant. "I grew up ridin' and handlin' animals on the farm. After the war, I went to Texas. They needed cowpokes, didn't care what color they was. Ended up here."

I wanted to ask more, but didn't know what was polite and what was nosy. My grandparents' hired help had once been slaves too, but I'd never thought about their lives before the war. This man seemed different. Freer. His need to get away from Virginia was, I realized, powerfully different from mine.

Just then Luke rode up, leading a big sorrel gelding.

"Found a bridle for you but no saddle. You okay bareback?"

I nodded.

"The remuda stampeded with the cattle, and we lost half of them. Too bad this horse wasn't one of them." He handed the bridle reins to me. "The others have their hands full. They got to round up strays. Let's hustle, now, so we can get the herd moving. Them Herefords are mixed in all over. We're going to have to ride in slow and rope them gentle. You coming?"

I clambered onto the sorrel's back, and the sorrel right away lowered its head and gave a sharp buck. The ground rushed toward me, too hard, too fast. Behind me I heard Mick snicker.

"He'll do that," Luke said. "Just give him time."

My stomach and head spun. I got up and staggered toward the horse again, hoping I wouldn't throw up.

I knew some horses would allow only one rider, no matter how well trained they were. Grandfather had told me how, as a young man, he'd tamed a stubborn horse by tying a blindfold around its eyes before he mounted. I patted the horse along its neck, spoke to it soothingly, and took a deep breath. I draped my handkerchief across the sorrel's eyes, then tucked the ends under the bridle to hold it in place. The sorrel reared its head, but I held it until it quieted and then swung onto its back. The horse stood perfectly still.

"That's how it's done!" Luke called. I slipped the handkerchief off and rode after him.

I couldn't have said what was going through me right then, mastering a horse in front of horsemen like these, swinging a lasso, riding with cowboys out on the prairie as the sun rose. I would have fought anybody in Virginia for that chance.

There must have been nearly two hundred long-horns spread under the shelter of cottonwoods along the creek, resting in the grass. Here and there, mixed in, I saw a red coat and white face—my herd. When the cattle saw us among them, they began to get to their feet, tossing their heads. "They're still jittery from yesterday," Luke said. "Take it real easy."

I rode toward a Hereford and her calf, but a longhorn in front of me jumped, scaring a cow next to it, who began to bellow. The entire throng of cattle surged forward. "Best we leave them Herefords in there today," Luke called. "The herd's on the hoof now, and we'll have a hell of a time cutting your cattle out without spooking the rest." He pulled a blue neckerchief up to cover his nose, motioned me to ride to the rear, and trotted up to the front of the herd, pointing them in the direction of the trail.

I had no choice but to follow. I guided my horse to the back. The other cowboys, when they saw the herd moving, gave up the hunt for strays and took their positions.

Mick, in a wide-brimmed felt hat and leather chaps, joined me. As we rode he explained how the cowboys drove the longhorns. Luke and Shorty rode at point, at the front and to either side of the herd. If Luke rode toward the cattle in front, they'd turn away from him and head toward Shorty, and that was how they guided the herd. Oscar and James rode swing, at either side and toward the midsection. Ben, the wrangler, stayed behind the herd with the remuda.

"And the lucky ones, us and Lightnin' Jack"— he pointed to the cowboy at the end of the herd opposite us—"get to eat dirt in the drag, back of the herd. We prod the stragglers." He turned toward me. His eyes, peeking out above his yellow bandanna, were ringed black with dirt.

I puffed up with pride. Even if I was riding drag, the least glamorous spot, I had entered a world that had existed only in my mind before, a shining place of dirt and freedom.

The wind blew the smell and the dust from the herd back toward me. I tied my handkerchief around my face, covering my nose and mouth, but my neck still itched from the dirt that seeped in. The stillness of the prairie was broken only by the lowing of the longhorns, the dull plod of hooves on grass, and the calls and whistles of the cowboys.

We were headed southeast, south of where the stampede had come through, and much farther south of home. Once in a while the cowboys would yell, "Hi yip! Hi yip dogies!" to keep the cattle moving. Midmorning, a longhorn in front of us stumbled and shoved through the herd, tossing its head, and galloped off across the plain. Oscar, ahead at swing, took off after it, and Mick gently trotted forward to take his place, to keep others from following.

Cowboy and horse seemed to be one animal as they chased the longhorn. They tried to cut in front of it to circle it back, but it dodged. Quick as a blink Oscar's lasso was up and out, and the rope landed over the neck of the steer, pulling the sliding knot tight. The horse stopped short and the rope stretched taut from the saddle horn. The steer bellowed. The horse circled behind, keeping the rope tight, as the steer, pulling away from the cowboy, headed toward the herd. At the herd's edge Oscar galloped up to the longhorn and with a quick motion loosed the knot from its neck, deftly avoiding the horns. He pulled his horse clear, coiled his rope around his saddle horn, and coolly took up swing again, while Mick rejoined me.

I was full of admiration for Oscar's work, but Mick snorted, "Fool hadn't ought to have roped him. Could have lost an arm, or stampeded them again, the way that steer was bellowing. I don't want nothin' like we had yesterday. Still, most of the time they walk slow as the devil, like this. Slow enough to put a man to sleep. I reckon you need a little excitement now and again."

It had never occurred to me that a cowboy's life might get boring.

"This herd is only the cattle bound for market," the cowboy continued. "After this, we move the rest to winter range." He cocked his head to one side and looked at me. "Where you live?"

I pointed toward the northwest. "Two miles west of Sweetwater Creek."

"You got Herefords? 'Bout twenty?"

I nodded.

"You ought to know better than to graze them on the range. Best keep them in that fancy fence you all are putting in everywhere over the country."

"We can use open range, same as anybody."

"And look what happened. Look at the fix you're in now. You farmers, come in and chew up the rangeland, get in the way." He lifted up his neckerchief and spat.

Had this been the Virginia schoolyard, I would have punched him. But I had noticed the long-nosed pistol in its holster tied to his thigh.

"You ranch outfits can't just run over anyone in your way. Nobody crowned you king of the prairie," I said.

He lifted his hat and swept it toward the herd. "But I am the king, and these are my sweatin' subjects. Look at 'em bow before me." He clamped his hat on his head and laughed.

I tried to ride farther away, but he stayed next to me.

"We was headed to Caldwell to the railroad, till this bunch took it into their heads to mosey somewheres different." Evidently he hadn't had a new person to talk to for a while, and he was ready to chatter. "This herd's half wild—we been out rounding 'em up along the Chikaskia for the better part of a month. Still, these critters musta known what they was in for—Chicago slaughterhouses at the end of the line."

"You're not Texas cowboys?"

"Texas? Hell, no. This is the Parsons outfit."

These were the cowboys I had seen, spurs flashing, riding at the edges of my life on the farm.

"I talked to Parsons' daughter, Evie. She wanted to ride this drive," I said.

The cowboy grinned. "Papa won't let her ride with the likes of us. Last time we was in, we was havin' some fun with a dance hall gal. Shooting at her feet to make her lift her legs higher. We wasn't going to hurt her none. Well, in comes the sheriff to spoil the fun." The cowboy's eyes darkened. "When the smoke cleared, I seen a friend of mine laying dead on the floor. But justice was done all right." He patted his pistol in its holster. "That ol' sheriff was laying dead right there next to him."

The cowboy dropped back after a longhorn that was lagging. I was glad to be away from him, glad Evie wasn't here around a man like that. I thought he was pulling my leg, but his talk, true or not, made me uneasy. Cowboys were supposed to shoot bad men, not sheriffs. All the cowboys wore pistols, but I had the sense he was more ready to use his than most.

Chapter 15

We reached Caldwell shortly before dusk. The longhorns balked at going into either of the two split-rail cattle pens at the edge of town, beside the railroad station. I helped press the herd close, so the longhorns would squeeze through the gates, my cattle among them. The cowboys had to chase down cattle that broke free from the herd. The townspeople, when the cattle herds came to town, evidently stayed indoors, out of range of longhorns that took off down the street with a cowboy galloping close behind.

I told Luke what the cowboy had said about the sheriff. "Watch out for Mick," he said. "He's liable to spin some fancy tales; but fact is, last year when our outfit came to town, a man ended up dead. I ain't saying how, but you steer clear of those saloons tonight."

"Just one man?" I thought that dozens of men died in saloon fights. They had in my novels.

Luke was startled. "That's one too many."

"Why isn't Mick in jail then?"

"I ain't saying it's him. Ain't saying it's anybody, but sheriff ain't a popular job in Caldwell these days, and nobody can make an ornery cowboy behave if he don't want to. It's a damn shame. If they didn't want our money so bad, the good folks of Caldwell would be right put out."

Mr. Parsons was waiting at the cattle pens. "Well, well, suffice it to say I wasn't expecting to see you here," he said when I rode up. He frowned when I explained what had happened.

"It will be difficult to separate your cattle at this point," he said, after a pause. "I'll tell you what I'm willing to do. You will get more money by selling the entire herd now and buying calves to pasture this fall. They may have contracted disease from my longhorns anyway. Let me sell the cattle for you, and you can take the money home to your parents."

Taking money home appealed to me. My family needed money. Also, there was no way I could herd twenty cattle on foot all the way back home, which was more than thirty miles away. "How would you know what price to sell them for?" I asked.

Mr. Parsons hooked his thumbs in his vest. "We'd rope one of your cows and one of your calves. Weigh them. Multiply their weight times the number of cows and calves you have. Figure the price by the weight, so much per pound."

Something was out of place here, but I didn't know what. His eyes, while he spoke, never met mine directly. He had never apologized for the trouble his herd had caused. I wasn't sure what to do. Mr. Parsons had been the first to help look for the little Weinhardt girl. And Evie Parsons, well, she was all right. But Papa didn't like Mr. Parsons, and I had a bad feeling about him now.

"I'd better get this herd home to my papa, thanks just the same," I said.

"Boy, it's two days on foot. You're better off selling them to a man who knows what he's doing."

His words made sense, yet I didn't trust his manner. He was already moving off, toward the livery stable, as if his decision must be law to a thirteen-year-old boy.

Papa had planned to wait until next year. I couldn't see how selling our herd now to buy more calves later would bring us more money. I decided I didn't trust Mr. Parsons.

"We want to sell the calves next year, when they're bigger," I said. "And we're keeping the cows to increase the herd."

Right then I knew I'd hit something. Mr. Parsons' face turned purple, and I thought of the cowboy saying, "You farmers, chew up the rangeland and get in the way." Mr. Parsons wanted our herd off the range.

"I'm sorry," he said. "There's no way to separate your cattle at this point."

Luke rode up then. "Fitzgerald," Mr. Parsons said. "Everything set for the evening?"

Luke nodded. "I'll be heading out first thing after the cattle are loaded tomorrow," he said.

"You sure you won't change your mind? I can't talk you into coming back with me?" In an undertone, Mr. Parsons said, "I'd make it worth your while. We'd have lost the herd if you hadn't been there. The others are idiots."

"Beg pardon, but they'd be a lot smarter with more pay and better food," the cowboy said. "No sir, my mind's made up, thank you anyway. Evening." Mr. Parsons' face froze as he watched Luke ride toward the livery stable.

I cleared my throat. "Mr. Parsons, I don't need to trouble your cowboys. I'll cut my cattle from your herd in the morning." I don't know what made me think there was any way a boy like me could handle twenty cattle in a herd of longhorns. Maybe I just wanted to stand up to Mr. Parsons.

Mr. Parsons' face gradually darkened, like a storm cloud gathering. He turned toward me and suddenly began to laugh, a harsh *haw-haw*. "Well, now, you're a right smart fellow. You better come with me to the hotel. Don't want your parents to worry."

But he paid no more attention to me, and I rode off instead to stable the horse at the livery. The sorrel, who had been fine on the trail, stopped just short of the stable and kicked. He backed up and tried to head downtown. I circled him around and around, trying to get him to go the right way. I got off and tried to lead him in. No luck.

"Here, greenhorn, let a real rider do it," the livery man said. I saw the cowboys exchange glances, and then saw the man go flying as the horse bucked him off. Laughter erupted around him. "Who's the greenhorn, you say?" Lightnin' Jack called.

I led the gelding to where the stable shaded part of the yard. I'd figured out that he got frightened when he saw the shadow of someone getting on his back. In the shade, with no shadow to worry him, I swung up easily. "You show him," Shorty yelled.

I rode the horse around the yard, let him see the pen, but he still didn't want to be confined. I got off again and tried bribing him with a pail of oats. "Come on, it's just for the night," I cajoled. "In the morning you'll be free as ever." He wasn't interested.

By this time a large crowd had gathered. "Here, youngster, try this," Lightnin' Jack said, tossing me a green apple.

I patted the horse. "Look," I said, holding the apple on the flat of my palm under the horse's nose. He sniffed, then delicately, with his front teeth, bit the apple in half. I held the uneaten part in front of him as he munched and lured him into the stable. I brushed him down and gave him an extra pail of oats before I headed for the hotel.

I followed the cowboys to Main Street, a block from the station. Caldwell looked much like our town. Unpainted wooden storefronts still the ashy color of new lumber lined the dirt street, reflecting the red-orange glow of the sunset. We passed an unfinished bank, a dry goods store, and a blacksmith, where bellows blew an open fire under the forge. Down a side street, away from the ordinary businesses, I heard loud voices and piano music. Caldwell was booming as the latest stop on the cattle trail. My father once, when he saw me staring after the cowboys, had told me how Kansas towns fought each other for the cattle trade, printing advertising bills and giving cash to herd owners to lure their herds. Wichita stole the business from Abilene and Ellsworth, and Caldwell took it from Wichita. Now the wild neighbor to the west, Dodge City, was making its own bid for the cattlemen, but so far Caldwell held on. My father had shaken his head, as if the whole business was crooked.

At the three-story brick hotel, Mr. Parsons gave the cowboys their pay in cash, and they headed toward the barbers for their first bath and shave after the trail. I lingered around the stuffy lobby, then sat on its fussy chairs and plush velvet settee, drawn by the good smells coming from the kitchen, until the bellboy noticed my dusty clothes leaving prints on the seats and shooed me away.

Dinner at the hotel was crowded with businessmen in black suits, traveling salesmen with stiff mustaches, and the cowboys, freshly combed and dressed. There was fried chicken, mashed potatoes and gravy, hot biscuits and butter, and cherry pie for dessert, all served on fancy china. The table reminded me of my grandparents' in Virginia. Their house seemed suddenly close, just at the other end of the rails.

A tired-looking lady in a striped skirt and a dirty apron kept bringing platters of food from the kitchen. Through the swinging door, I could see flies buzzing around the uncovered food. Flies buzzed in the hot, airless dining room too, landing on the rims of crystal goblets and on shiny tops of heads. Mr. Parsons talked loudly and clapped men on the back as he ended his stories. His voice made my head ache. I pushed back my plate, stood up, and walked toward the door.

The lady took hold of my elbow and steered me toward a room with a porcelain basin and pitcher on a washstand. "Clean yourself off before you get into bed," she said. "Get some clean clothes, too." She said the cowboys bought a new suit of clothes when they got to town, and usually threw the old ones, dirty from months on the trail, into the rubbish heap.

"I don't have money for new clothes," I told her.

"Put it on Mr. Parsons' bill. He's got credit at every store in town when the cattle come in. If you're with him, you can bill it."

I thanked her. After I washed up I sauntered down the boardwalk to the general store, exaggerating the bow of my knees so folks would know I'd been on the trail. The store sold everything from canned food to nails to calico, and stayed open late when the cowboys came to town. I picked out a white cotton shirt and black pants, the first new clothes I'd had since coming west. A tan felt cowboy hat, with a wide brim and a leather band around the high crown, caught my fancy. Boss of the Plains, it was called, made by the Stetson company. But it was expensive. I didn't want to be that indebted to Mr. Parsons.

I wore my new clothes out of the store, carrying the dirty ones rolled like cowboy bedding. Mattie could wash them; there was no use in throwing them away. I started for the hotel, but heard the music again and decided to investigate.

Jammed into the side street I'd seen earlier were about a dozen buildings, brightly lit, some with false fronts. The door to the nearest was open, but there was no music. Eight or ten men,

Mick and James among them, slouched silently at a bar, which was only a plank of wood on some sawhorses. The men and the bar filled the tiny room.

Next door, a much larger room had a mirror at the back and rows of colored bottles behind a polished wooden bar with a brass foot rail. The men from the cattle drive, including Luke, were playing poker at tables scattered around the room. A half-empty bottle sat in front of Lightnin' Jack. A woman in a blue silk dress and a black hat played lively songs on a piano at the front.

Back home in Virginia, in Youngstown, there was a tavern where Grandfather stopped now and then for ale, and I had gone with him and drunk cider. Men had talked politics and smoked cigars. This saloon was far noisier and drunker, much like I had imagined the saloons of the West would be. In my imagination, they had been strange, exotic places. I went in eagerly.

I went to the bar and ordered a whiskey. The bartender said, "Son, we don't serve children here."

"Just a cider, then."

"Got no cider. Go on home, now. The drys would skin me alive if they thought I was corruptin' a child."

"Who are the drys?" I asked.

"The meddlesome holier-than-thous, temperance folks. They're already pushin' the prohibition laws to put me out of business." He turned to a salesman slouched at the bar. "But if I go, the cowboys go with me, and their money with them." The salesman raised his glass of whiskey in agreement, and the bartender refilled it. He saw that I still lingered at the corner of the bar. "Go on, now."

The look on his face told me not to argue. I stood up my full height and scowled, but I left anyway. My father didn't have any liquor on his place, and I'd never seen it at the Alsatian neighbors', but I'd never thought to wonder why not, and I'd never heard talk of drys or prohibition. Evidently I'd stumbled on another battle I knew nothing about.

As I walked through the swinging doors back out to the dark main street, I bumped against Mick and four other men I didn't recognize, all wearing spurs and cowboy hats. They paid no attention to me as they pushed inside. I slumped against the wall of the saloon, not wanting to go back to the hotel but unsure what to do next. Luke strode out, pocketing a wallet. "Hey, partner," he said. "Where you going?"

"Just trying the saloons," I said. I hoped he hadn't seen me inside. I didn't want him to know I'd been told to leave.

"You go on back to the hotel, now. Things can get rough around here, real quick." Luke glanced down the street. "I'll help you get your cattle in the morning." He patted my shoulder and walked off in the opposite direction, past the row of saloons where people called out from the brightly lit doors. I watched him turn the corner and decided to follow. He entered the dark alley behind the saloons, where a row of narrow, one-room houses waited, each lit dimly or not at all. Several men were in this alley. They passed one another without speaking.

The cowboy went to one of the unlit houses and knocked. I hid in the shadows, watching for what seemed like forever. I was tired, but if I left, I'd miss knowing whatever was there that made a man give up the lights of the bars to stand in the gloom, all alone. Finally, a small glow appeared at the window, the door opened, and a man walked out. The cowboy and the man didn't speak or look at each other as the man passed by. Then there was a flutter at the door, and a woman stood there. She and Luke spoke softly, briefly, then she took his hand, led him in, and shut the door. The light went out.

These houses never appeared in the dime novels. I realized with a shock what they were, and who the women were. At the cowboys' campfire I'd overheard one of the cowboys talk about "getting to a crib" when he got to town. This was something dark, hidden. I felt ashamed being there, watching.

My own loneliness hit me then, so dark I couldn't see any way out of it. I felt far away from anyone who cared about me. For a moment I considered knocking at one of the other doors, wondering what would happen. What were the women behind the doors like? What had brought them here, where even in this open country they had to be shut in darkness?

After a time, I turned and headed up the street toward the hotel.

I thought of my father and Mattie as I walked. For the first time, I wondered about the years my father had been out on the prairie alone, after my mother died. I wondered if he was all the more lonely for having had someone and lost her. Then Mattie came, with a family. I began to forgive my father, a little, for marrying Mattie, if she made him less lonely.

Chapter 16

The sound of gunshots woke me in the night, four or five, one after the other in methodical rhythm, louder and more frightening than I could have imagined. I pulled my pillow over my head until the blasts stopped. When I uncovered my ears I heard shouting. I hunted for my boots, trembling as I pulled them on.

Downstairs in the street there was uneasy quiet, no one about. The air smelled smoky. I ran across the dark alley to the next street, where the saloons were, and saw people huddled at the door of the saloon I'd been kicked out of earlier. Footsteps pounded down the boardwalk and the crowd gave way to a man with a bag, the doctor.

I followed behind. Inside, a man lay on the floor, his head propped against the piano at an odd angle. The piano player in the blue dress knelt beside him, pushing the folds of her skirt against his chest to stop the blood spreading on his shirt.

The crowd around me crackled with anger.

"It was a setup."

"This is the third one this bunch has shot. Now ain't you ready to do something about it?"

"What are we going to do? I'm a doggone grocer, not a gunfighter."

"He never saw it coming."

"Time to get the U.S. marshal down here, or the army."

The doctor felt the man's pulse, reached in his bag for bandages.

"He ain't dead."

"Not yet. It don't look good."

"How's this town supposed to get anywhere with these ruffians shooting the lawman every year?"

For the first time I saw the badge, smeared with blood, on the man's chest. "Who did it?" I asked.

"One a them cowboys come to town. The gang done took off. It's the same ones as last time, I'll wager, just working for a different outfit."

I looked at the people in the crowd. They weren't customers, but townsmen who'd run from their homes in their shirtsleeves when they'd heard shots. Some hadn't bothered to tuck their nightshirts into their trousers. None of them were cowboys from the drive.

Two men came from a back room carrying an old door, which they loaded the wounded man on, gently. "Easy, deputy. We'll get you home now," they said as he moaned. They carried him out and down the street. The doctor followed. As they passed me, I blanched at the sickly-sweet smell of blood, and the gray, twisted face of the hurt man.

A short man in a bartender's apron sat down at the piano and the music started up again, hollow-sounding now. People began to walk away. I was grateful for the cool night air out in the street.

I went back up to bed, my heart still beating hard. The rest of the night, try as I might, I couldn't close my eyes without seeing a spreading pool of blood, shaped like a tear.

As soon as gray light filtered into the sleeping dorm, I got out of bed, picked up my roll of dirty clothes, and tiptoed past the snorers, stepping over the ones who hadn't made it to bed. Outside, in the morning chill, the town slept. The wide dirt streets were empty, and meadowlarks sang out on the prairie.

The cattle were quiet in their pens by the rail-road station. I leaned against the fence, trying to think. The confusion of the night still echoed in me—the sound of shots, the sight of the blood, the dark alleyway and the shadowy faces. I pressed my forehead hard against the wooden rail, feeling the scrape of the rough splinters.

The honorable thing was to get my cattle and get home, away from this place.

The train would pull up in a few hours. No one was near now, except a railroad clerk buried somewhere in the train station. What if I opened the gates, chased all the cattle out of the pens? I could see them running down the main street, into the blacksmith's yard, up the steps of the church, smashing glass, crashing through boards into the homes and businesses of the very people who treated Mr. Parsons like a king when he came to town. That would fix Mr. Parsons. What a fine mess!

But my father would surely make me pay the damages, and there would never be money. Besides, I'd likely lose my cattle, and the reason I was there at all was to get them home.

I went to the livery stable for a rope. My cattle weren't wild. If I could get the cows out, one at a time, the calves would follow and they would just graze nearby while I got the rest. I made a lasso, went around the pen to the nearest cow, stood on the bottom rail, and tossed the lasso toward her, figuring to lead her out of the gate while I stayed safely outside the pen, out of range of those horns.

Well, I missed on the first toss but got her on the second.

I should have realized she wouldn't like the rope. She jumped as it landed around her neck, pulled as I pulled, and I toppled over into the pen.

I got out of there quickly, having landed too close to longhorn hooves for the second time. The cow wandered to the center of the pen, the rope trailed after her, and her calf bawled beside her. I rubbed my shoulder, which I'd bruised when I fell. Maybe I could get another rope and try again. Maybe she would wander close to the fence and I could grab the rope.

"Good morning."

I felt a tap on my sore shoulder and spun around. Mr. Parsons stood there, smiling. "I thought I'd find you here when I didn't see you at the hotel." He held a bank note out to me. "Two hundred dollars," he said. "Estimated value for your herd. All yours."

I looked at the note. It was made out to me: *Pay to the Order of Thomas Hunter* was scrawled across the paper in fancy handwriting.

"Take it, son," Mr. Parsons said.

This was a direction I hadn't expected from him. A boy like me could never hope to have that kind of money. Two hundred dollars would buy a horse and a good saddle. I could make my way to Texas or Montana, go with Luke maybe, work for a big ranch. Two hundred dollars would more than pay for a train ticket to Virginia, as well.

Two hundred dollars was also what my father had paid for the ten Hereford cows a year ago. I had asked, and written it down in my journal. They were worth more now, because they were fatter, and there were the calves also. I didn't know specific cattle prices, but I guessed the herd had to be worth twice two hundred dollars. And it would be more valuable next year, when the calves were grown.

I made my choice. I took the bank note.

And I tore it in half, then in fourths, then eighths, and I tossed it toward the sky and watched the pieces flutter down. "I aim to get my herd and head home, with your help or without it," I said.

"You're making a foolish decision. Your family needs that money."

"I'm not going to steal from my family, or let you. They need the cattle."

"Thomas, be reasonable. We can't separate the Herefords from the longhorns."

I hadn't worked cattle long enough to know if this was true, but I didn't say anything. I went to the stable for more rope, and for the next hour tried to lasso my cows, without any more luck than I'd had on my first try. Mr. Parsons watched me the whole time, hoping, I guess, that I'd give up and agree to sell, and after a few more bruises and a kick in the shins I wasn't sure but what I might.

Luke and Shorty arrived then, to help herd the cattle onto the boxcars. "It's just me and Shorty helping you," Luke said. "The others disappeared, real mysterious, after the deputy got shot last night. Except Jack, who's sleeping off his whiskey." He said this casually and went to work right away, but I saw the spot on his new shirt where he'd tried to wash out a bloodstain.

At least I knew now that Luke hadn't pulled the trigger. I wondered how close he'd been to the bullets.

I wasn't scared by how near I'd been to the violence. If anything, I was disgusted. I knew that from then on, when I saw a cowboy riding in the distance, I would see the silver flashing and wonder if it came from a killer's gun.

About a dozen others arrived to wait for the train also. Everyone wanted to watch the spectacle of the cowboys and the longhorns.

"Why no," Luke said when I asked him. "It ain't hard to separate them if they behave. Those pens are built so's you can separate your herd. We'll just load one pen at a time and head your Herefords off into the other, instead of up the chute to load." I told him then about Mr. Parsons' bank note, and why I didn't take it. He didn't say anything, but he nodded, and I could tell he approved.

Mr. Parsons strode over. "We'll load *all* the cattle," he ordered.

Luke rubbed his forehead, closed his eyes. "Mr. Parsons, we can separate those Herefords for the boy—if that's what he wants." He opened his eyes and looked directly at me.

"I do," I said.

"Well, if you are sure," said Mr. Parsons, and *he* looked at me, hard.

"I am," I said.

"Right," Parsons said, glancing around at the crowd of watchers.

I expected a much bigger fuss, but instead he became concern itself, even offering to help as the train arrived, whistling and blowing black smoke, scaring the cattle.

The cattle quieted by the time the train was ready to load, the slatted boxcars positioned so that the open doors of the first car lined up with the loading chute of the pens. Luke put himself at one of the gates, and Shorty, on horseback to rope strays, stationed himself at the other. Mr. Parsons found he had business in the depot. I ran to help Luke, and we swung the gate of the first pen open just wide enough to let a cow into the chute. The cattle backed away, but as Luke prodded with an iron poker, standing nearer to those horns than I ever wanted to, they scrambled one at a time up the chute into the dark car. Some of them swung their horns in the chute and got stuck, and Shorty would dismount and help Luke wrestle the animal free. Some of the cattle fell going up the wooden plank and entered the boxcar limping. I could hear them in the car bawling, hooves thudding on the metal floor, and I could see them dimly through the slats, milling in confusion. The air began to smell of the stink they made in their fear.

Four of my Herefords, with their calves, approached the chute with Luke's prodding, and it was, as he said, not hard to steer them into the other pen, with Shorty guarding the gate. About five longhorns went with them, thinking they were headed for freedom, before Shorty could close the gate and Luke could prod the longhorns toward the chute. One boxcar filled and we waited while the steam engine fired up, blasting steam, to pull forward a few feet and bring us the next boxcar.

In all truth, getting my cattle went smoothly, except for the cow who decided she'd rather see Chicago than go with me. She scrambled up the chute with the longhorns before we could turn her.

Real quick I threw my arms around her calf, who was ready to head up the chute behind her. I tossed him to the ground, surprising him and myself, and held on as he kicked and squirmed and bawled.

This put the cow in a dilemma, whether to abandon the boxcar or the calf. As she hesitated at the top of the chute, Luke poked her with his iron, and she made up her mind and slid and stumbled back down.

We loaded one pen, then the other, and finally the longhorns were on the train and the door of the last boxcar was slammed shut and locked. All of my Herefords stood uneasily in one of the pens. The watchers had boarded the train or met their loved ones and gone home. I dusted myself off as the train prepared to leave the station. Mr. Parsons walked over to me.

"By the way," he shouted over the noise of the steam engine, "this may interest you. I'm purchasing the Judson place."

In my life I was to meet many whose politeness masked their greed, but Mr. Parsons was the first, and he truly shocked me with his duplicity. He meant that the Judson place, where we grazed our cattle, would no longer be free rangeland. In other words, I had to keep our cattle out.

He walked back to the hotel as the train pulled out, saying, "My best to your parents."

I looked for Luke and Shorty, but they had gone. Quiet settled over the pens as the train grew smaller in the east. Its clamor dwindled and died long before it left my sight.

Only then did I let myself consider what I had to do to get the cattle home. They would be hungry, and it ought to be easy to herd them out onto the prairie, but once out there I didn't know if I could keep them moving. The farthest I had ever herded them was two miles, and I had at least thirty to cover, providing I could find the way. If they scattered, how could I round them up?

I went to the livery stable. If I could still get Mr. Parsons' credit, I could rent a horse. But the man at the stable told me the credit ended when the train left town.

Well, that meant I couldn't get any food either, and I was hungry after the morning's work. It seemed there was nothing to do but get started.

As I was opening the gate I saw Luke walking toward the pen, leading the sorrel gelding. He handed the bridle reins to me. "You solved my problem," he said. "You're the only other one can ride this gelding, and I can't bring him with me to Montana. I can't sell him because he's got a reputation. So I guess you'll have to take him, till I get back to these parts anyway. Look after him good now for me, you hear?"

I didn't know what to say. I just stood there, hoping my face said thank you, because words couldn't begin to show how grateful I was. A thirteen-year-old boy couldn't weep with relief and joy in front of a seasoned cowhand. Hugging and dancing were probably wrong as well.

"I'm headed to Montana on the evening train," he said. "The westbound. Otherwise, I'd help you get that herd home."

He helped me prod the cattle out of the pen and walked a distance with the herd, until we came to the creek that I could follow to the Chikaskia River, which would lead me back toward home. He gave me a roll of beef jerky, which he said he had left over but which he had likely just bought for his train trip.

He stuck his hand out to me, and I shook it, proud to do so. Once more, for the briefest flicker of a moment, I thought about asking to go with him to Montana. He was the point where my dream of the West and the real West met, and I was glad to have known him.

"Thank you," I said.

"Take care of that family," he replied. He walked back toward town. I never saw or heard from him again.

Chapter 17

Two days later, at dusk, I brought the cattle home.

The farm looked different, though I was hard pressed to say how. The chickens still scratched in the dirt, the logs of the low house remained weatherbeaten.

Two nights on the prairie on my own, driving cattle along the river across thirty miles of prairie without losing any, wasn't what made the difference, even though I had a pretty healthy respect for myself as a cattleman now. The difference was that I saw the place without any halfway feeling, without thinking I might be here or I might be gone.

Mattie was spreading laundry out on the grass to dry. She dropped the clothes back in the wooden washtub and squinted, wiping her hands on her apron. Emma stopped weeding in the cornfield and ran to meet me.

"Thomas, where have you been? We thought you took the cattle and cleared out to Mexico."

Poor Emma. The one who would likely tell if she caught me not working. A permanent frown etched her face already.

"I've been rounding up the cattle, Emmabean. And I brought a horse home for us."

"Why did you lose the cattle? We thought you were gone for good." This must have been an echo of Mattie. She didn't anger me, though. There was worry behind the words she parroted, and she was too young for worries of that kind.

"The cattle were run off by a stampede, Miss Emma, but I saved them. And I rode beside cowboys with hats bigger than you. One of them gave me this horse."

Emma followed as I herded the cattle into the corral. "Mama was plenty mad when you didn't come back."

"I imagine she was." I dismounted. Mattie had turned away and begun spreading clothes on the grass again. I walked over to her, leading the horse. Emma trailed behind.

"Where's my father?" I asked.

Mattie jerked her head toward the south. "Plowing. With Caleb."

"I brought the cattle home."

"I can see that. You took your sweet time about it."

She hadn't changed while I was gone. But I no longer wanted to argue with her. Her hands, red from scrubbing clothes, made me feel sorry for her, a little.

Mattie was not someone made for pity. "You'd better not have stolen that horse, that's all I have to say. I won't have the law out here after you."

"It was a gift."

"From a cowboy," Emma said. "After the stampede."

"You got mixed up with the stampede," Mattie said, stopping her work.

I told her the herd had been swallowed by the runaway longhorns, and I'd gone to Caldwell to get them back. I described how Mr. Parsons had tried to take our herd, and how I had stopped him. And I said Luke had given me the horse.

"People don't give away perfectly good horses."

Praise from her was too much to expect, but I resented her scorn. I didn't tell her how Luke was. I didn't care to hold my memory of him up to her inspection. I said he took the train to Montana and couldn't sell the horse.

"What's wrong with it?"

"Nothing."

Mattie continued to scrutinize me, suspicious. "Your clothes are different," she said at last.

I told her Mr. Parsons had paid for them, and for the hotel.

"Just why would Mr. Parsons be so generous?"

"He wanted to buy our herd, I told you. For half of what it's worth. He wanted to get our herd out of the way on the range." I was telling the truth, but from the hard way she stared at me I felt I was lying. I hoped Mr. Parsons wouldn't demand that our family repay him. "I brought my clothes back." I took down the bundle I had slung in a roll over the horse's back.

"Well, I've just done the washing, so those will have to wait," Mattie said, but the scorn had left her voice. She eyed the gelding. "Show the horse to the barn. It'll mean extra shoveling in the morning."

Mattie would expect the worst of anything, even a gift. I watered the horse at the trough and spread dried grass on the floor of the barn for him. I'd become very fond of him on the way home, and had tried without success to think of a name. I patted his nose. "This is it," I told him. "You're home."

I washed up at the bowl outside the house, running the rough cloth over my neck and scrubbing my face, then dried off slowly. My stomach was hollower than it had ever been, but I was reluctant to go inside with Mattie.

The smell of chicken frying drifted to me. Mattie stuck her head out the door. "Company dinner tonight. Your father's been worried."

That was all she said. She ducked her head back inside. Company dinner—fried chicken was for special occasions. For me, she meant, in the language of the place, where gestures stood for words. This was her way of offering . . . what? Surely not peace. Respect, maybe. I smiled, and told myself to remember to compliment her cooking.

I stood in the doorway scanning the prairie until my father walked over the ridge with Caleb. Papa saw me, but his expression didn't change and his step didn't quicken. I hung back, unsure. He came up and hugged me, the first hug since I'd arrived from Virginia.

"Where the hell have you been?" he asked.

"I had to go cowboy," I said. "Mr. Parsons' long-horns stampeded our cattle, took our herd clear to Caldwell. Mr. Parsons wasn't sorry it happened, either. Papa, he wants us off the range."

Papa nodded, unsurprised. "I rode out looking for you, found where they'd stampeded. Wouldn't have been the first time someone got hurt. How the hell did you make it back in one piece?"

Over dinner I told my story, how I'd dealt with Mr. Parsons and how Luke had given me the sorrel gelding. I mentioned the gunfight, but left out the part about the trip to the houses in the alleyway.

"We heard that the deputy got shot down there," Papa said. "If I had known a son of mine was there, I'd've been out after those cowboys. They been running things in Caldwell too long."

I was pleased to think my father would have defended me.

"He was out trying to find you two days as it was," Mattie said. "He let the chores go. You'll have to help him catch up."

That night, the bed felt more cramped than usual after my open-air beds under the stars. My muscles ached, my hands were sore from the rope, and my feet were blistered. Yet for all the discomfort, there was a satisfaction I'd never known before. I had survived, had been honest, and above all hadn't lost any cattle. I had "quitted myself like a man." That phrase came back to me from *The Pilgrim's Progress*, read in a stifling schoolroom in Virginia, years ago it seemed, in another world.

Chapter 18

A cold spell in October curled the leaves on the pumpkin vines in the garden but left the plants unharmed. Then the days were hot again, but with a difference: a dryness in the air hinted of change to come, and the mornings were cool and still.

Another letter came from Becky, and a letter from my grandparents for my father. I read Becky's driving the wagon home from town, where I'd sold butter and eggs to the town women and bought husking gloves and corn sacks for Papa. I let the reins go slack, and the team followed the meandering road on its own. The letter gave greetings from my grandparents and then surprised me with news:

> You remember I wrote of my friend Ida, with whom I spent part of the summer? Her brother John and I

have exchanged several letters since then. In his last, he proposed marriage, and I accepted.

She told me I'd like him, that he worked with his father in a grain-shipping business in Norfolk, and that they would live in that city after they were wed. They planned to marry when he'd saved enough money. "I know you'll be back by then," she wrote.

She assumed I'd be back. Of course, I wanted to attend the wedding. But this news showed me how far the distance was between us. Her life would be Norfolk society, presiding over teas and giving to charity, whether I was there or not.

I tried to picture what Becky would have been like if she had come with me. In town, maybe, she could have been happy. I couldn't see Becky marrying a German farmer or a cowhand, though, or living Mattie's life.

The image of Evie Parsons riding over the prairie came to me, with her tied-up skirt and bright copper hair, collecting buffalo bones to buy her own cow. What Evie did interested me more than what Becky did, I had to admit, even if Evie had the wrong father.

If I went back to Virginia, even to visit, would I become the boy I had been, punching at every imagined insult and living by some kind of make-believe code of behavior? Or would I bring the real West back inside me?

The next day Papa said it was good corn harvest weather. I had never harvested corn before. While Caleb and Emma helped Mattie chop the ears from the stalks, I helped Papa husk. We sat on wooden stools out in the cornfield, ripping the green husks until the yellow ears, stringy with corn silk, dropped out. We tossed the stripped ears into bushel baskets and the husks in a pile on the ground, to save as fodder for the animals and kindling for the stove in the winter.

As dusk drew near Papa and I worked in silence. Lately silence between us had become comfortable. But that night I sensed that something troubled him.

Finally he looked up at me. "Your grandparents want you back, to go to school," he said.

I tensed. My grandparents always wrote as if I'd be returning someday, but I hadn't expected them to appeal to Papa so soon. I had written them after I got back from Caldwell, on pages torn from my journal because we had no writing paper, and told them about finishing *The Odyssey* and keeping the journal. I'd minimized my trip to Caldwell; emphasized my new horse, whom I'd named Wanderer; and told them about our plans for breaking sod and fencing this winter and selling cattle the next fall.

I also told them about baby Jacob's death and how sad I was about it, a sadness that I felt more since I'd come back from the stampede. Every time I was out on the prairie now, I picked wildflowers to lay on his grave as I returned. If they were telling Papa to send me back, they must be worried that I was less and less inclined to go.

"You can't go to school out here this term," Papa was saying. "You want learning, you best go back. For good."

I pulled an ear of corn from the bushel basket and dug my fingers in deep.

"They sent a ticket this summer. Now they're insisting," Papa said.

I kept busy with the corn, jerking at every green strand. "What do you think I should do?" I asked at last.

"Not having learning is a hard thing," Papa said. "I wouldn't keep you from it, if it was up to me. There just ain't the opportunity here yet.

Someday, but not now." He was turning an ear of corn over and over in his hands. "The harvest work is about done," he said. "I can spare you better now." Papa threw the ear of corn into the basket. He rubbed his hands on his pants legs. "This place is hard on children growing up. You could have been killed several times on that escapade of yours. I don't know if I was right to bring you out here."

"Why did you, then?"

In the rows of the cornfield I could hear Mattie: "Just the biggest ones, Emma. How many times do I have to tell you? We cannot waste corn picking unripe ears."

"It's a hard life," Papa said, gesturing toward them. "You learn that young. It never stops being hard. You work and you work, and you think someday it'll all be worth it. Keeps you going. Then the wheat prices fall. The crops fail. You start to get old, and you realize you're working as hard as when you started." He stared at me. I shifted uncomfortably on the wooden stool.

"I just wanted you out here with me, you and your sister," he said. "I thought now that Mattie was here, I could take care of you properly." He raised his arm in a sweeping gesture, out toward

162

the prairie. "This wouldn't be right for Becky. For you, though, I thought maybe it would be right." He stood, turned away. "But I don't want to keep you back, Thomas. I don't want to take away your chance because of my stubbornness."

I was glad to hear him say he wanted me. I hadn't always been sure. I ran my finger along the plump kernels of corn, thought of how good the crop was since the rains. I thought of what I wouldn't have to do if I went back: get up before dawn, muck out the barn, work from morning to night in heat and cold, wear mended clothes and too-small boots, live with a stepfamily. I thought of being near Becky and my grandparents again, having all I wanted to eat, going to the academy, wearing stiff uniforms, studying the same as my grandfather had, and his grandfather before him. I thought of what I would miss: my horse, the wildflowers that I could name in any direction I looked, the rough sacks of buffalo bones that brought the first money I ever earned, the stars spilling across the night, the cattle I chased at dawn over the prairie, my papa, my step-family. I saw he was waiting for an answer.

"Well, I wouldn't have to get up so early if I went back," I said. "But who would muck out the barn?"

He smiled then, the biggest smile I'd seen on him, and he picked up an ear of corn and went back to work husking. "There will be schoolteachers, you know. You will have to go sometime or other."

"It won't be the same as reading Homer out on the prairie."

Papa smiled again, more thoughtful. "You know that won't last forever. This corn crop should buy us enough barbed wire to finish the fence before it snows, if we hustle. One of these days fence will be up all over this country. Won't be no open prairie."

I tried to picture fences running at right angles to one another across the prairie in every direction. I couldn't imagine there ever being enough fence to cover the prairie, though I knew he was right.

But for now the grass waved far out beyond the cornfield. Wildflowers nodded, and I heard the mourning dove coo as the last rays of the sun turned the sky golden pink. Whatever this place was not, whatever it took from me or demanded of me, it offered itself in return.

Author's Note

This is a might-have-been story based on family history. My great-grandfather really did come from Virginia to Kansas twice: first as a baby, the second time in the 1880s at the age of nine, to live with his father and stepfamily on the Kansas prairie. Let me share some facts about historical things mentioned in the novel.

Railroads came to this part of Kansas throughout the 1880s. In fact, their coming brought more farmers to the area and heated up the conflict between the farmers and the cattlemen, who wanted to keep the open range.

The railroad came to Caldwell in 1880, making it a shipping point for cattle from the Chisholm Trail cattle drives from Texas, as well as a shipping point for area ranchers. Caldwell was already a violent town because of its location on the Trail—according to one source, eighteen marshals died in Caldwell between 1879 and 1885. The townspeople became more and more frustrated with the violence, lynching one outlaw in 1881.

Caldwell had one dance hall, which was also a brothel, brought to town from Wichita in 1880. A boy like Thomas certainly would have seen it—it was on one of the town's main streets. Cattle towns tolerated brothels, because they made the cowboys take baths and spend money; but townspeople didn't like them, so brothels often were housed in less visible areas, such as the Crib Row in the novel. I created a

Crib Row for Caldwell because it's a lesser-known aspect of cattle towns than the saloons you see on TV and in the movies. Selling liquor in saloons was supposed to be illegal in Caldwell in 1881, because of an amendment to the Kansas Constitution passed that year, but saloon keepers continued to operate as long as they could get away with it.

I made Thomas's father a little different from other Kansas farmers in that he planted spring wheat instead of winter wheat. Farmers at that time didn't know what kind of wheat would grow best in the area. The kind for which Kansas is famous—Turkey red winter wheat, brought by Mennonite immigrants in the 1870s—wasn't widely planted until the 1900s. Spring wheat was planted sometimes, but as Thomas's father found out, it didn't grow as well here.

Children growing up on the prairie faced many dangers. Before the invention of vaccines, children were more likely to catch infectious diseases such as whooping cough (pertussis) and diphtheria, and many children died of these illnesses. The story of the lost girl, Marie, is based on the true story of a girl from western Kansas who got lost on the prairie during the winter of 1890. But Elliott West, a historian who has studied children of the American frontier, writes that in spite of all the dangers prairie children faced, they were actually no more at risk than children in other parts of the country, and in fact may have been safer. However, he says, the parents of frontier children who died almost always felt guilty for bringing their children to an uncertain new country.

The Alsatian immigrants, although they spoke a German dialect, would be French immigrants if they came to Kansas today. The Alsace-Lorraine region went back and forth between French and German rule. In 1871 Alsace-Lorraine was made part of Prussia, which today is part of Germany. Prussian authorities made life difficult for Catholics and Evangelical Protestants in that area, so many of them immigrated to the American plains, along with thousands of other German-speaking people. Alsace-Lorraine became part of France again after World War I.

The verse the cowboy sings in Chapter 13 is from a song called "The Kansas Line," a cowboy folk song from the late 1800s.

Sources

Primary:

Colt, Mrs. Miriam Davis. *Went to Kansas: Being a Thrilling Account of an Ill-Fated Expedition to that Fairy Land and Its Sad Results.* Watertown, N. Y.: L. Ingalls, 1862.

Garland, Hamlin. *Boy Life on the Prairie.* New York: Harper & Bros., 1899.

Ise, John. *Sod and Stubble: Story of a Kansas Homestead.* Lawrence, Kans.: University of Kansas Press, 1970, 1996.

Reiley, Josephine Moorman, ed. "I Think I Will Like Kansas: Letters of Flora Moorman Hesston, 1885–86." *Kansas History* 6: 2, Summer 1983, pp. 71–95.

Roosa, Alma. "Homesteading in the 1880s." *Nebraska History* 58: 3, Fall 1977, pp. 371–94.

Spitzli, Otto. "My Lot in Life" (Family memoir). 1954. *Wichita Beacon*, August 4, 1880.

Secondary:

Brumfield, Kirby. *The Wheat Album.* Seattle: Superior, 1974.

Butchart, Ronald E. "Education and Culture in Trans-Mississippi West." *Journal of American Culture* 3: 2, Summer 1980, pp. 351–73.

Cather, Willa. *My Antonia.* Boston: Houghton Mifflin, 1918.

Coburn, Carol. *Life at Four Corners.* Lawrence, Kans.: University of Kansas Press, 1992.

Doig, Ivan. *Dancing at the Rascal Fair*. New York: Simon & Schuster, 1987, 1996.

Dykstra, Robert. *The Cattle Towns*. New York: Knopf, 1968.

Fink, Deborah. *Agrarian Women: Wives and Mothers in Rural Nebraska, 1880–1940*. Chapel Hill, N.C.: University of North Carolina Press, 1992.

Freeman, Craig C., and Eileen K. Schofield. *Roadside Wildflowers of the Southern Great Plains*. Lawrence, Kans.: University of Kansas Press, 1991.

Hampsten, Elizabeth. *Settler's Children: Growing Up on the Great Plains*. Norman, Okla.: University of Oklahoma Press, 1991.

Halsell, H. H. *Cowboys and Cattleland*. Nashville: Parthenon Press, 1937. Reprint: Ft. Worth, Tex.: Texas Christian University Press, 1983.

Haywood, Robert. *Victorian West: Class and Culture in Kansas Cattle Towns*. Lawrence, Kans.: University of Kansas Press, 1991.

Kansas State Cooperative Extension Service. *One Hundred Years of Progress in Wheat Production in Kansas* (pamphlet), 1977.

Kingman County, Kansas 4-H Council. *Kingman County: A Township-by-Township History*. 1977.

Milner, Clyde A. II, editor. *Major Problems in the History of the American West*. Toronto: Heath, 1989.

Miner, Craig. *West of Wichita*. Lawrence, Kans.: University of Kansas Press, 1986.

Nelsen, Jane, editor. *A Prairie Populist: The Memoirs of Luna Kellie*. Iowa City, Iowa: University of Iowa Press, 1992.

Owensby, Clenton E. *Kansas Prairie Wildflowers.* Ames, Iowa: Iowa State University Press, 1980.

Raban, Jonathan. *Badland.* New York: Random House, 1996.

Rounds, Glen. *The Cowboy Trade.* New York: Holiday House, 1972.

Sandoz, Mari. *Old Jules.* Lincoln, Neb.: University of Nebraska Press, 1935.

Sedgwick County Extension Education Service. *Native Grasses of Kansas* (pamphlet), 1997.

————. *Twenty Selected Kansas Wildflowers* (pamphlet), 1994.

Stoecklein, David R. *Cowboy Gear.* Ketchum, Idaho: Dober Hill, 1993. The cowboy song is an actual song taken from this book.

West, Elliott. *Growing Up With the Country.* Albuquerque, N. Mex.: University of New Mexico Press, 1991.

West, Elliott, and Paula Petrik, editors. *Small Worlds.* Lawrence, Kans.: University of Kansas Press, 1992.

Wister, Owen. *The Virginian.* New York: Signet, 1979.